JOY RIDE

JOY
RIDE

BARBARA HOWELL

VIKING

VIKING
Published by the Penguin Group
Viking Penguin Inc., 40 West 23rd Street,
New York, New York 10010, U.S.A.
Penguin Books Ltd, 27 Wrights Lane,
London W8 5TZ, England
Penguin Books Australia Ltd, Ringwood,
Victoria, Australia
Penguin Books Canada Ltd, 2801 John Street,
Markham, Ontario, Canada L3R 1B4
Penguin Books (N.Z.) Ltd, 182–190 Wairau Road,
Auckland 10, New Zealand

Penguin Books Ltd, Registered Offices:
Harmondsworth, Middlesex, England

First published in 1989 by Viking Penguin Inc.
Published simultaneously in Canada

10 9 8 7 6 5 4 3 2 1

LIBRARY OF CONGRESS CATALOGING-IN-PUBLICATION DATA
Howell, Barbara.
  Joy ride.
  I. Title.
PS3558.0896J69   1989   813'.54   88-40397
ISBN 0-670-82653-7

Printed in the United States of America
Set in Garamond No 3.
Designed by Sarah Vure

Each life converges to some centre
Expressed or still;
Exists in every human nature
A goal

EMILY DICKINSON

THIS BOOK IS FOR MY SISTERS,

Virginia Howell Byrnes
and Stephanie Howell Larkin.

JOY RIDE

ONE

Joy has found a new man she says will save her. And maybe he will. Her life has always been cyclical. Just as you think she has reached the final stages of self-destruction and dreariness from which no woman ever returns, up she pops again, riding the crest of whatever big-spending, high-rolling wave is passing through.

She claims it is sex that is keeping her and Scott together. Supposedly it's never been so riotous, frequent, tender and sweatily energetic in her life before. Which is ridiculous. She got him with her fame and writing talent. From the beginning, their relationship has been mired in desperation and opportunism.

Consider the circumstances of their first meeting. Consider a slightly overweight, round-faced woman with blond, wispy hair framing her face like alfalfa sprouts. She is in a room two thirds full of women. The other third consists of married men and a few neutered bachelors: lost souls with mottled freckled hands, crusted with callouses and spongy noses sprouting broken capillaries. It is a tenants' meeting in Joy's rent-controlled building on West 107th Street near Broadway.

They are assembled in the lobby—cracked tile floor, bare vanilla walls except for a couple of depressing smoked mirrors. The only furniture: two elaborately gilded, much-glued Louis XIV console tables that look like they came straight from a whore's bedroom, with spindly gold-painted chairs at each end. The other chairs, rented for the occasion, are of the folding steel variety with that special slant that's guaranteed to dislodge the coccyx after sitting in them for twenty minutes.

The noise is deafening. Everyone is shouting at the leader of the group, a relatively educated Irishman who relocated from Riverdale to Manhattan when he left the mother of his children and took up with a stiletto-heeled manicurist who is currently squatting in a sunny four-room railroad apartment, bequeathed to her by her mother, who squatted before her. For less than $150 a month. The group views her Irish lover as an intruder and they are doing their best to dethrone him with demands to have the floor and much scratching of their steel chairs.

Joy, who is too irresponsible to care what happens to her apartment, barely hears the bedlam around her. She has no desire to influence the meeting. She has no money and whether the rent rises or falls or the building goes co-op is of no concern to her. Her only goal is to find a man who will get her out of West 107th Street.

After writing one bestseller and three lesser books and spending all the money she made on them without giving any of it to the Internal Revenue Service, she is deeply in debt and perilously close to going to prison for tax evasion.

She would like to write her way out of her predicament and has filled fifty pages with words of an inchoate, narcissistic nature to this end, but she fears she really doesn't have another book in her. She fears that her talent (for that's what she had—getting people to pay for your books, no matter how revolting they are, requires talent) has been slowly seeping out of her for years. Her former publishers and agents seem to share this view.

Consequently, she knows she must employ her other considerable gifts to achieve her goals, which, aside from the desire to relocate to a better neighborhood, are fairly modest. All she wants is to be able to buy a couple of outfits from Yves Saint Laurent twice a year and go to a good restaurant two or three times a week, where she will be recognized as a famous writer and have a fuss made over her. After that, well, anything can happen. With good food in her stomach and a Saint Laurent outfit (no matter how inappropriate for her current shape) on her back, she can carry on to the grave, enjoying her fading fame and keeping anxiety (of which she has a good deal) at bay.

She surveys the crowd dispiritedly until her eyes, which are of the yellowy-gold, wandering variety, land on a dark-haired, broad-shouldered man in an expensive suit. Her heart lightens.

She makes her way over to his side of the room. With a gentle shove here, a timid excuse there, she is soon within whispering distance of him. Except for his nose, which is a trifle bulbous, his large-boned face vaguely resembles that of Gregory Peck.

"I don't know if I can stand much more of this," she says, as though he were an old friend whom she has known for years.

He nods in a manly, attractive way and ignores her. This excites her interest more. For she is well aware of her un-prepossessing appearance. Though her round, even-featured face is still rather sweet, her attire—corduroy pants and an old cashmere sweater (the YSL outfits are strictly for non-building events)—is not up to standard for a man of his caliber. Her eye makeup, put on at noon, is probably smeared or nonexistent. Worse, her hair, which hasn't been cut in months, is a mess. Were he to pay court to her right away, there would be something wrong, something too needy, about him.

She gazes at him fixedly during the hush which follows a large Puerto Rican woman's announcement that she cannot put a penny more than $50 toward the hiring of a lawyer to defend them against their landlord.

The other tenants are aghast. It never occurred to them that they would have to hire a lawyer. They thought their careworn, television-tired brains were sufficiently agile to get the better of their heartless, greedy landlord, who, in addition to having an MBA from Fordham University, has two mistresses and a wife, whom he houses and feeds without any of them knowing of the others' existence. Joy, who has talents along somewhat the same lines as the landlord, shakes her head indulgently. For the truly stupid, she is always compassionate. It's smart people she likes to sharpen her teeth on.

"Do you live in the building?" she asks sweetly.

"Yes," he replies without interest. His face has no expression. It is as tedious as a granite wall.

"What floor are you on?"

"Six," he replies.

She nods sagaciously in the manner of one who has just retrieved some historically important information.

"I'm on five," she says after what she believes is a sexy little pause. Which it is.

His left eyebrow moves up as he looks down at her adoring, vulnerable golden eyes. Forget the decadent little puffs beneath them, the soul of an eleven-year-old burns through those eyes. Then, slowly, like a timid sun breaking through a gentle autumnal cloud, a smile lights her face.

"What's your name?" he asks.

"Joy Castleman," she replies.

The name doesn't register. He is not a reader and even if he were, it would never be of women's fiction, that much is clear just looking at his jaw.

What is this well-dressed, virile, affluent man doing here? Is he just staying at a friend's place because his wife has taken the kids to Martha's Vineyard? Is he a spy for the Fordham-educated landlord? Is he on his uppers? Does he too owe the IRS his life and what's left of his soul?

"What's your name?" she asks.

"Scott Arnold."

Easy to say and easy to remember as names go. Joy Arnold sounds good too. She smiles again, looking even more vulnerable than before. She has given me this smile. If, like me, you're a woman, you want to hit her. If you're a man, you want to violate her and maybe hit her too. But you do neither. You already feel guilty and she is already winning, but you have no idea of this.

"God, it's stuffy." She sits on a folding chair near him and fans her face with her hand, the fingers babyishly splayed, so that the least possible air is circulated. Her hands—soft and smooth with barely visible veins and buffed, well-shaped nails—are an important feature.

"I wish they had a drinking fountain," she says and sticks out her tongue a half inch to indicate its parchedness and waits while an invitation to have a drink in his apartment percolates inside him.

She has learned long ago that inferiors, if they are to be trusted and liked, may be the first to speak to a superior, but must never extend the first invitation.

I became aware of the wisdom of this view while riding an escalator in Altman's. Two stunningly dressed women—one black, one white—who worked in the store were ahead of me, chatting gaily about this and that. And I thought, How nice that, at least in the middle classes, racial prejudice has diminished. Then I heard the black woman say, "Give me your phone number and I'll let you know when it's on. We can go together." To what? A film? An art exhibit? I'll never know. The point here is that the white woman—same age, same lithe, well-jogged figure—stiffened and a deeply reflective expression passed across her face. The black woman had broken the rule that the inferior must never initiate the first date. This is the white girl's prerogative. The black must wait to be chosen. If she does not, she risks being labeled pushy, maybe even dangerous. In any case, not trustworthy.

Now Joy has always believed that women must behave as though they are men's absolute inferiors. It was one of the first things her mother taught her and has served her well. This belief is the root of her remarkable success with men and the fountain from which spring the good meals and YSL suits, as well as, in good years, weekly massages, trips to the Caribbean in the winter and typists. For she also knows that, for the right to consider themselves more intelligent, aggressive, daring and steadfast than women, men must pay. And pay and pay.

"Would you like to come up to my place for a drink?" he asks politely, but with the usual condescension accorded by men of his age and class to unattached, fortyish women who approach them.

She ignores the manner and jumps at the words. In seconds she is on her feet and both of them are threading their way through the heckling tenants. They take the elevator, paneled in steel and painted a cigarillo brown. On the inspection sticker are scrawled the first names of most of the tenants' offspring.

By the time they leave the elevator, she has learned that he is a business consultant, which probably means unemployed, but she doesn't care. She definitely smells money coming from somewhere.

While he fumbles with his keys, she lets him know: "I kind of write."

He drops the keys. Bliss! He is impressed. He is possibly even scared!

Like blacks who sing or dance or play ball (to pursue my

tiresome analogy with our fellow inferiors), women who write or do anything in the arts, while definitely lesser than male artists, are nevertheless fearsome to ordinary white men. They are even more terrifying to men who have undeveloped artistic leanings of their own.

Striding through the door first, picking up an overcoat draped on the foyer table, his back to her, he asks, "What have you written?"

"Just four novels."

"Should I have read any of them?" He looks down at her patronizingly, regaining some of his previous control.

She lowers her eyes modestly. "Maybe. One was a best-seller."

He looks quizzical. To him, all best-selling writers are millionaires. What is she living in this dump for?

She understands the question in his eyes. She is wondering the same thing about him, but it is too early to go straight to finances.

She slips around him and enters the living room. It is furnished with two brown sofas and a desk piled high with bulging manila file folders. What looks like an antique Kelim rug is rolled against the longest wall. Three unhung pictures lean against another wall and a dozen cardboard boxes are scattered about which serve as side tables. Near the window is a large François Premier–style chair with nicely carved feet and arms which looks like one of a pair.

"Just leave your wife?" she asks.

His face registers amazement at her perspicacity. "Not exactly. Or yes. Actually, maybe."

"Was it awful?"

"Not particularly. It was mutual. A mutual parting of the ways." His voice is brusque, but his eyes, which are darting all over the place, betray still-fresh bewilderment over his new single condition.

She looks down as she steps over one of the cardboard

boxes and smiles to herself at the thought of the nice little challenge he will present.

"It's hard to get apartments in this building. How did you manage it?"

"By paying the real tenant three times more rent than he pays. He's in the Bahamas."

"Was his name Mackenzie? I remember a John Mackenzie with a beard. I think he was on six. Kind of an investor?"

"No, he has another name."

"Does the landlord know he's subletting?"

"Of course not. We're at your mercy." He flings his arms out in an attitude of mock desperation. But they are strong, muscular arms and the look he sends her is (to her) interestingly menacing.

"Don't worry about me. I'm getting out of here as soon as I finish my next book."

Again the look of mild terror crosses his face. "What would you like to drink? I have everything. Cointreau, brandy, Grand Marnier . . ." As he speaks he is opening one of the cardboard boxes and pulling out dusty, half-filled bottles that look like they were bought a decade ago in a duty-free shop. He is obviously not a big drinker. Neither is Joy. Another thing her mother taught her is that men hate a drunken broad. And since all good things flow from men, one must never become something they hate. She also does not smoke.

What she does do secretly is take pills, many pills, but it will be months before he learns about them.

All he will learn tonight is that she is not only a writer, she is a willing muse and mentor, and possible gateway to the fame and fortune he longs for.

For he is indeed trying to be a writer himself. Sitting primly on the brown sofa with her pretty hands folded on her lap, ignoring the thimbleful of Cointreau he has poured for her, she gradually gets him to reveal that he has written sixty pages about his youth and two hundred or so about the breakup of his marriage while looking for work.

Unfortunately she was right about his being unemployed. He has just recently lost his job as the division manager of a large cosmetics firm and must spend a good part of his time sending out letters and résumés and having job interviews. But whenever he has a free moment, he is writing the whole, violent, tension-filled tale of his wars with Marisa.

For that is the name of his immensely wealthy former wife. A name that, for Joy, is easy to hate. The very enunciation of it conjures up someone slim and spoiled, living on a large estate with acres of lawns and carefully tended flowerbeds. Someone given to ruinous, joyless shopping sprees and long, treacherous silences. Someone who, I might add, will never become Joy's victim.

By ten-fifteen, she has got him flipping through a file folder, thick with expensive typing paper, and admitting how much writing means to him.

She says he must believe in himself and never stop writing. She can tell, just listening to him—the way he expresses himself—that he has great sensitivity and a keen eye. As reflected in his choice of, er—her eyes drift around the room for confirmation of this last superfluous compliment— paintings.

She lavishes praise on the brownish abstract paintings leaning against the wall. He says he knows very little about modern art and looks flustered. Noting his confusion, she figures that Marisa chose them and, considering the mood she was probably in when they parted, they are very likely the worst paintings in her collection.

She moves quickly on to other aspects of his wonderfulness. Even his stance demonstrates his forcefulness. "You know what I mean? The way you walk. The way you kind of put your chin out when you talk." It proves that he has the courage and stamina to be a great, great writer, better than she will ever be.

She flatters him mercilessly. He tries desperately not to preen. His knuckles are turning white as he grasps the claws of the armchair.

She waves away his offer of another drink, drops the names of world-famous writers she knows personally and rhapsodizes on the thrill of being a Real Success.

His jaw softens. He is weak with longing to enter that celestial world of names. For in a godless universe, are they not the only idols worth mentioning? Plus they only work a few hours a day and don't have bosses and people ask them for their autographs. Plus they are rich.

But is he? Before the night is out, she must get the answer to this question. Not that it matters that much. He is a find, no matter what his income. If nothing else, he could be an excellent escort for the smoke-filled, lavishly hors d'oeuvred West Side publishers' and writers' parties she still attends, whether invited or not. But he would be an even greater find if this whole maneuver could end with him supporting her.

His present wealth will also determine whether or not she will acknowledge his timid hints that she "take a glance" at his work, which, he confesses sheepishly around midnight, is "rather voluminous." He hasn't written 260 pages. More like 2,000. Those aren't business files on his desk, as he had implied earlier, but his total oeuvre. All of it unedited. Full of a freshness and purity he never perceived in himself before. It is the Real Him. The truth about him.

She nods comfortingly. Being twice as smart as he, she knows he is incapable of putting the truth about himself on paper. No man married to a woman whose name is Marisa would ever know the truth about himself. Also, his suit is too well cut.

Ever so gently, she nudges the conversation back to money. By one A.M., she learns that he is living off the interest on his savings and that Marisa is not asking for alimony. In addition to having a Ph.D. in anthropology from Columbia University and writing scholarly articles in anthropological journals, she is the heiress to a cereal fortune accumulated two generations ago in the Midwest. Their two sons, one a law student at Yale, the other just starting a career in investment banking, are the beneficiaries of trust funds set up many years ago by their maternal grandparents.

Considering his former job and the small amount of money he was probably required to contribute to Marisa's household during their marriage, Joy figures that his savings are in the neighborhood of $500,000, which, invested at 10 percent, would yield about $50,000. After taxes (which a man like him would pay), he most likely has about $35,000 a year. Not much. But if she could get him working again, he would surely be able to earn from $100,000 to $150,000 a year.

But to get him sufficiently infatuated to pay her back taxes of $217,000—it is a dream, but why not dream it?—she must convince him that he is a great novelist whom she can mold and edit. But how can she make him go back to work if she is also convincing him that he is a great writer?

A problem of timing here.

Which she feels confident she can solve.

At three A.M. she decides it's definitely worth the trouble to take two big files, containing approximately three hundred pages each, down to her apartment. She promises to read them the next day. She has nothing special to do. In fact she is a little "blocked." She needs the stimulation she knows she will get from reading the work of a real man's man. Somewhere along the way she has decided he is a man's man. He likes the sound of that.

Bent over from the effort of carrying a file under each arm, she raises her sweet, expectant face to him. He kisses her lightly on the mouth, but she feels the hungry vibrato under the surface of his lips. She knows he would like to rape her right there, but among other inconveniences—he is tired, she might sue him—his precious unpaginated work would scatter everywhere and who knows if it could ever be put back in its original, pristine order.

Day two finds them back in his apartment. It is six P.M. Books from seven of the twelve cardboard boxes have been placed on the bookshelves in the living room. There are various atlases, some boring novels, a complete *Encyclopaedia Britannica* and several books on how to write.

Both are sipping diet cola. She has read the first twenty pages of the six hundred he gave her and has found it to be the sludge she expected it to be. Nevertheless, she has discovered many things about him. Namely, that his favorite adjective is "beautiful," that his conformity and self-control are limitless and that there is little hope that any of it will ever be published.

"You're great," she says, crossing her legs gaily. She is wearing an antique, carefully ironed, tummy-hiding white lace Victorian nightdress with a ruffled cotton petticoat beneath it. Around her neck is a velvet ribbon accented with a tiny cameo brooch. Whenever she moves in for the kill, she dresses in clothes recalling bygone days of virtuous, disease-free women with fragile wills and tremulous, unmentionable needs.

"I think we can turn you into a real writer," she says in her high, babylike voice. One of Joy's verbal mannerisms which I've forgotten to mention is that, as she has grown older, she has trained herself to pitch her voice an octave higher than it used to be.

Possibly she thinks it compensates for her widening waist and appalling street smarts. Possibly she's right. In any event, we can safely assume that Scott is not put off by this infantile vocal style. He is too busy struggling to control the exultation, relief and pride that is surging through him upon hearing her words of praise.

"There are a couple of people I want to show your book to," she says.

"Really?" He tries not to smile, but the corners of his mouth have backed up to his ears.

"One is an editor at Knopf. He would like your kind of hard-nosed writing."

"Hard-nosed?"

"You know. Tough. Do you know what Knopf is?"

He shakes his head.

"It's one of the most prestigious of the big fiction houses. They do John Updike, Doris Lessing, John Cheever—all the greats."

"Incredible!" He shakes his head in wonder over her knowledge. "How do you have all those names at your fingertips?"

"You'll soon know all these facts yourself. Writing is a business like any other. I can teach you the basics pretty quickly."

She lowers her eyes. Words like "teach" do not come naturally to her. Her role is to absorb, or, more accurately, suck the life out of whoever happens to be her mark of the moment.

She touches her hair self-consciously. With the help of half a can of hair spray, she has swept it up in a turn-of-the-century mode with pale, tendrilous curls spiraling down the sides of her cheeks. "It will take time to pull it together, but I'm sure there's a bestseller here."

Glints of self-satisfaction are bouncing off his eyes as he watches her flip through the stack of paper and land on a page which, if it were paginated, would be around page 400. She scans it rapidly. "I love the part here—" she puts her finger on a few lines in the center of the page, "where you describe Marisa's throat. 'The milky strangulable texture of her skin' . . . I wonder if 'strangulable' is a word. Never mind, it's good. The minute you started describing her I wanted to strangle her. Did she really not know how to make a bed?"

"Barely. She didn't lift a finger in the house. The maids or the nanny did everything."

"Really?"

"She never cooked me a meal during our entire marriage."

"There was a cook?"

"God, yes."

"We had a cook too. I mean, my parents did when I was growing up. Meals were always a surprise." Her eyes meander over to his tidy efficiency kitchen and back to his virile, bony face. "Did Marisa really go to Cameroon to study those Pygmies for her doctorate?"

"Yes, she went there three times. They're called the Baka. They don't like it when people say 'Pygmies.' I should take that word out." He reaches for the page she is holding.

She stays his hand. "We'll edit later. Did she stay long?"

"A couple of months at a time. She wanted to learn their language."

"Did she leave you alone with the kids?"

"No. She only traveled when they were away at prep school."

"It sounds fascinating."

"Yes, if you think watching people gather and hunt and gather all day is fascinating."

"I bet being in the jungle was hard on her milky skin."

"Well, maybe it's not that milky."

"But over all, she's gorgeous, smart and rich, right?"

Joy feels her confidence ebbing. She studies his face to see if he is comparing her to his wife. She believes that when men are comparing an ideal mental image with the reality sitting in front of them, it always shows. He isn't. He is, thank God, still hating this wife-goddess he left such a short time ago.

She relaxes into the brown sofa's downy cushions (all the cushions in Marisa's home would of course be stuffed with real down) and feels her spirits lifting. "I like the part in the beginning of the book where you describe her excuses for not going to bed with you. Saying she has too much gas is terrific. That's realism. Another writer would have said she had a headache."

"It's true." His face lights up with delight at the marvelous conjunction of a true-to-life detail and art. All controls seems to have vanished from his consciousness. "After she went on a high-fiber diet, she was fixated on gas and constipation."

"It's very French to talk about excremental matters, very Rabelaisian."

His eyes turn wary. She realizes that suspicion is his automatic defense against any foreign name or intellectual concept of which he is ignorant.

Thus she goes easy on the Rabelais and doesn't even bother to explain who he is, suspecting that for him any writer who lived prior to Hemingway is dangerous territory.

This is a shame, since she has a well-deserved reputation for knowing about writers who dabble heavily in anal matters: Pauline Réage (the pseudonymous author of *The Story of O,* her favorite novel), de Sade, Norman Mailer and Henry Miller. One of the ways Joy made her name is through her fascination and familiarity with buggery.

That and her suffering.

Her success story is worth recounting here before describing the rest of their evening. (For by now you have guessed that, with Joy directing the action, it will end with them going to bed after he has taken her out for a three-hour, five-course meal in an overpriced restaurant of her choice.)

* * *

She has had a tumultuous life. To begin with, she was born into the rich bohemian world of the New York theater. Her late parents were Terence Claire and Maddy Bolingbroke, the celebrated acting team who succeeded in staying married for thirty years and raising four children. Joy was the eldest of the brood and the family blabber.

For not only has she written about the vast, multistaffed estate in New Jersey where she grew up in mesmerizing, consumer-conscious detail—brand names of cars and small planes, exact years of vintage wines, names of Paris dress designers frequented, even the Latin names of the rare flower bulbs, smuggled in from Europe, with which the gardens were planted—she has shared with thousands of readers all that went on in her family: the drug abuse, violence, illness, frequent incarcerations in mental homes and screaming at each other all the time.

Despite these irregularities, their house, which was right in the heart of the horse country in north central New Jersey, was always teeming with producers and directors. To hear Joy tell it, they couldn't spend a Saturday afternoon at home without a Jessica Tandy, Katharine Cornell or David Merrick dropping by. Everywhere you looked—in the bathrooms (all with their own phone and bidet), in the billiard room or lurking on the servants' backstairs—there were matinee idols, gods and goddesses.

Wealth and divinity hovered over their estate with such intensity it's amazing they had time to eat, sleep or make any money. In her long, spellbinding accounts, things like weather never happened either. It never rained or snowed. Every day they were bathed in perpetual, media-blessed sunlight.

Some of Joy's choicest stories were about the children of the stars. Not surprisingly, they were more precocious than most. The boys loved to gang bang her. She adored it actually, but, as time passed, she learned from her editors that she had been victimized and that, anyhow, victimhood made far better copy in commercial fiction. Thus she turned the considerable pleasure she derived from the entry of several cocks into her of an evening into an experience so agonizing, so gory, grotesque and enthralling that it was worth the price of the book.

After a while, boys bored her and she began to hanker after women. Probably even today women are what she likes best. It's difficult to tell about her real sexual proclivities. Her personality is like her literary style, which slips and slides around with so many picturesque, meaningless, paradoxical adjectives, parenthetical remarks and qualifying clauses, it is impossible to pin down what she really means or feels. Perhaps she feels and means nothing and is all flow. "Staying in the flow" was one of her preferred clichés during the sixties. And she does flow on.

(Though occasionally there's static. Especially while she's in the process of flattering you. Just as you're sinking into this warm bath of praise she's pouring over you, she will suddenly swat you with what I've come to call a "counter-flat." It is a sort of unconscious, deadly zinger that comes out like a Freudian slip, or more like an actor's aside to the audience which is—in this case—her secret banshee self.

One day she was telling me how beautiful, how efficient and warmhearted and, well, how just about perfect a wife I was, when suddenly I heard the words "like Agnes Moorehead used to be."

"Agnes Moorehead?" I gasped, remembering that she had played I don't know how many repressed spinsters, dour governesses and prison wardresses throughout her long, dreary acting career.

"Did I say Agnes Moorehead?" Her eyes widen with surprise as her pretty hand taps her forehead. She is such a naughty girl. "What am I thinking? I don't know what made me say that."

For the record, I am a tall, cheerful, red-haired still-life painter. Nothing about me resembles the dark, dangerous, harsh-voiced characters Miss Moorehead used to portray. But now that Joy has put that thought in my head, late at night, when someone hasn't returned a phone call or I've given a boring dinner party, it looms to the fore and I wonder if somewhere under my jolly carapace lurks a mean hag with dungeon keys jangling in her hand.)

Joy's resistance to classification, sexual or otherwise, however, is her principal literary strength.

No one ever knows exactly what she means. Unlike her speech, which is direct and slangy, she comes across on the printed page as opaque and impenetrable. You understand only every third sentence or so. A lot of people—and some reviewers—think this is class. I read somewhere that T. S. Eliot and Ezra Pound are responsible for this glorification of obfuscation in writing. Similarly fuzzy thinking seems to have infected our art critics. What other culture would put up with the boredom and bullshit of Minimalism? I could spend a long time railing against them for this, but it won't change the fact that artists who don't say anything significant are granted incredible respect and adulation these days.

In a way, it is understandable. For if we allowed plain thinking to infiltrate our minds on a regular basis, we would have to dwell on things like the venality of our political leaders, the Bomb, the anomalous position of women, the devastation of nature and other soluble problems we are determined not to solve.

Thus, it pays to stay dumb and praise what is so densely, blurringly written and blandly painted, it can't possibly motivate anyone to do anything about anything.

Though I must say that in Joy's writing there is always a strong narrative snaking its way through the phalanxes of adjectives which is vivid, violent and revolting enough to make you keep turning the pages.

You are especially fascinated because you're pretty much convinced that what she describes is autobiographical. Not only are her heroines' parents always famous actors, all her novels are in the first person. The photographs on the book jackets encourage this view. Her first book, *The Lost and the Mad,* had a picture of her peeking over a beach blanket in a flesh-colored bathing suit. Two straps are visible on her shoulders, but at first glance she appears to be naked and on a bed, not a beach. The half-open mouth and the wan, childlike expression in her huge eyes suggest such helplessness you find yourself believing that it's all true. That when only an adolescent, she really did have her anus repeatedly penetrated and ripped by two Irish lawn boys and one grease monkey in the back bedroom of her family's mansion, and that she truly did catch her mother in bed with a celebrated courtesan and join them, and that after leaving home, she personally spent a whole summer chained to a four-poster bed in the Beverly Hills home of a famous movie director noted for his sadism on the screen and in life.

The Lost and the Mad is a chronicle of her affair with this cruel director, who, in addition to making three movies a year, supplemented his income by dealing in drugs. After whipping and buggering her for a whole summer, he turns her into a "mule." This is someone who carries dope on planes and past customs officials in airports. Her run is from Marseilles to Paris to Los Angeles.

She carries the heroin in her vagina, wrapped in a condom. The description of its removal in the airport ladies' room (one must remove it as soon as possible, she tells us, because, if it breaks, one risks death) is appropriately graphic, vulgar and nauseating, but you read on—do you ever. You want her to get that glutinous, lethal mess out of her as quickly as possible because if she doesn't, she may die.

The death which she doesn't die has been described at great length before we get to the airport ladies' room: "the fatal flicker of life clawing at my delirious brain, gray with tremors and the fulsome music of the damned." You want her to live mainly because, if she dies, or even gets a little sick, you know you'll have to wade through a two-page re-depiction of fatal flickers.

Somehow she knows this, knows when she has adjectived you out and she plunges the story forward with several pages of readable narrative. The cops arrest her in the airport and take her down to headquarters. Handcuffed again, this time to a water pipe in the officers' urinal, she is raped by a Polish police sergeant and gets a "sly sloping pleasure" from doing it more or less upside down.

Throughout the book, she never condemns any of this male brutality. On the contrary, she seems to relish it.

The book closes with her getting out of jail, thanks to her father, the famous stage actor, who is a close friend of the governor of New Jersey. She settles down to paint moun-tainscapes ("stony monoliths, tethered together in their spir-itual isolation . . . sturdy symbols of my alienation . . .") in Taos, New Mexico. But she is resigned to a life of fear, since the sadistic boyfriend, who has conned his way out of a prison sentence, has been known to throw lye in his ex-girlfriends' faces, turning their lives and faces into "ambulatory leprosariums."

Anyhow, people adored it. She cleared about $400,000. The Book-of-the-Month Club made it an alternate selection, there was a big paperback auction, and *Cosmopolitan* cleaned it up and condensed it. Even a major movie production house took an option on it. Obviously, it never made it to the big screen, since all the good parts, even in this day of explicit disgustingness, were unfilmable.

TWO

Since I was not present during Scott and Joy's first encounters, I suppose I have no right to describe them, but she told me about them in such detail I feel as though I had been there. And after twenty years of knowing and being fascinated and repelled by Joy, I am fully capable of filling in the parts she left out.

My reasons for setting all this down are still obscure to me. Probably I am trying to figure out what Joy means to me or, more precisely, why her existence on this earth irritates me so much.

Why do I care? Why does she matter to me? Well, obviously, because she does. And oddly, inexplicably, so does this Marisa, whom she despises. I don't know exactly why they're important to me, but I will when I'm through. It's the same with paintings. When you begin, you don't know why some flower or piece of fruit is demanding to be painted, but toward the end, just as you're filling in the background, it comes to you. You find what you wanted to find.

I met Joy during the late sixties, right after I moved to New York from Saint Louis. Yes, I'm from the Midwest. The Great Midwasteland, the Bible Belly, Pitsville and so on, ad nauseum, if one listens to my New York friends. Forget our concert halls and museums, our ancient parks and stable aristocracy (on the fringes of which my family has maintained a respectable position for generations), New Yorkers will always think that their multicultural vulgarity and freneticism constitute some sort of classic ideal for living. So be it. When I came to New York, I thought as they did. And still do, in a way, on days when I choose not to think about the street crime and crack sellers, the child abuse and wife battering going on behind closed doors and the thousands of homeless on the other side of those doors.

We had our first conversation at the counter of the coffee shop in the midtown building where we both worked. She was a receptionist for a big publishing house and went by her maiden name, which was Claire. My name was Gibbons then. Madeleine Gibbons. I was an art director for a medium-sized advertising agency. There was some mix-up about our food orders, a brief exchange about the abysmal service and we were soon chatting together like old friends. She looked much the same then as today: a few pounds overweight, round, charming face, flyaway hair and gorgeous hands with perfect oval fingernails she buffed every day.

We had only twenty minutes to talk before dashing back to work, but in that time she managed to hint at the network of names which supported and nourished her bright young being, like some sort of powerful, immutable grid.

To my delight, she was at the counter the next day and we took up our conversation where we had left off. From then on, we began to meet regularly.

I was spellbound as, lunch after lunch, names of actors, directors and producers spilled from her mouth. When she learned I was interested in fine art, and wanted to become a real artist one day and not remain an art director forever, she revealed that she also knew several greats in the art world. Before his death, her father had often entertained Rothko and tried to get him off the booze and drugs. Her late mother had bought paintings from Leo Castelli, and Joy herself had gotten to know Jasper Johns one winter on vacation in Saint Martin in the Caribbean. What's more, Andy Warhol was a regular at the parties she attended.

Every tale, every word out of the mouth of this snub-nosed girl with wandering, gold eyes enchanted me. It astounded me that anyone so ordinary could come from such a glamorous background. But there she was, sitting beside me at the counter, pushing her tunafish salad around on her plate, while I, concentrating fiercely on all she had to say, felt myself getting more impressed, depressed and confused with every new revelation.

Up until then, I had been pretty full of myself. I do not mean this in a pejorative sense. By full, I mean brimming with a sense of my achievements. For I had managed not only to get a degree in fine art at the University of Missouri, but to leave home, find a job that didn't require typing and wrench myself away from the bleak religion I'd grown up with. Though I still loved Roman Catholic ritual and the medieval and Renaissance art it had engendered, I'd begun to have glimmers of a larger, happier vision of women than Christian doctrine afforded. Perhaps this was because, for the first time in my life, I was having fun.

I adored the craziness of the sixties, having my own place— a shabbily furnished three-and-a-half-room apartment on East Twenty-fifth Street—and all my New York friends, mostly professional and semiprofessional young men and women from out of town like myself, who loved parties and believed they were more liberated than any Americans before them.

I relished every minute of my independent, New York life (I fervently endorsed the idea of "living in the present") and was confident of my ability to cope with any and all problems that might come my way.

A few lunches with Joy reversed this.

In her skillful, beguiling way, she opened my eyes to a larger, more powerful, sophisticated world "above" me which she penetrated regularly. Through her, I came to see that, although I spoke well, enjoyed above-average intelligence and looked great in my boots and minis, I was basically a no one, unblessed by notoriety, great wealth or high-achieving parents, who thought of everyone who peopled the tabloids as Them and everyone I knew as Us.

In truth, the most famous person I'd ever met was Senator Eagleton (the 1972 vice-presidential candidate who had to withdraw when people discovered he had had shock treatments). And I hadn't even really spoken to him, just pressed his hand as he was walking off the golf course at the country club where I was my best friend's guest. I'd also gone to school with the daughter of Sam Sloane, a Missouri disc jockey, and I had, like most Saint Louis nice-girls, danced with and been propositioned by a member of the Busch clan.

Up until then, it had never occurred to me one could do things like goad Margaret O'Brien into a temper tantrum, swim in a swimming pool with Arthur Miller and sit at the dinner table and ingest food with Katharine Hepburn's bony face chewing three feet away from yours, as Joy had, so many times, over and over, all her life, actually.

And I, dumb predictable little girl that I was, felt my heart beat with gross expectations of one day meeting these luminaries through my new friend, Joy, and perhaps advancing myself as an artist, courtesan, slave girl, whatever.

Now that I am older and have had some experience with the desperate hype of the SoHo art market, I'm aware of the fragility of fame and know that Names are low-grade currency, mean very little to other Names and have power only over non-Names.

I also realize that Joy's name-dropping number with me was not unlike the average publicist's introductory skit when he is soliciting business. She differed from publicists, however, in one major way. She wasn't offering her services. She was breaking her back to impress me so I would service *her.*

She was only twenty-two when I met her, but she had already worked out a very efficient survival system for herself, whereby she got the maximum money and services out of her friends, lovers and acquaintances for the least amount of effort expended. So effective was this technique that it transcended any discussion of women's inequality.

If she saw any likelihood of your being useful to her, she directed a simple three-pronged attack which had you groveling at her feet in record time and begging for the right to give her whatever she wanted from you.

First she would establish her credentials—illustrious father, mother, friends, etc.—then, to draw you in deeper, she would sweeten this starry pudding with tales of scandal: about an actor's wife who seduced a famous producer's wife in a steam bath so her husband could get work or about a world-class director's daughter who witnessed a shoot-out between her parents. She was especially entertaining when describing gruesome surgical operations: Marlene Dietrich's face, so lifted and tightened she could ingest food only through a straw; P———, who was born without a vagina and tried to have one made in a seventeen-hour operation which failed; Z———, who had a clitorectomy to please her jealous lover.

Self-mutilation, drunkenness, violence, unfettered ambition, they were all there. All the sins! Oh what a sorry lot they are, you think contentedly. Worse than anything you've ever read about. Ten times more wretched. One hundred times more vain, weak and insecure *than even you are.*

After a while, she has you so completely under her spell and puffed up with feelings of superiority over these unfortunate stars, whom lesser clods, those who don't know Joy, still look up to, that you don't stop to think about what you will do with these fulsome inside stories. Tell other people; "I have this friend who knows everyone, who told me that

J——— has intercourse only with women who pee on him"? Not a bad gambit while waiting for another round of drinks in a slow bar, but not anything valuable. Nothing you can sink your teeth into and use to further your career or importance in the world. You're not a witness to any of these perverse actions she describes. You're not even an acquaintance of the perpetrators. You're just a gossip repeating another gossip's story.

But you don't realize the valuelessness of the data right away. You're still licking your chops over the deliciousness of just *knowing* how depraved they all are when she comes on with the second phase of her attack.

She starts slowly with an account of her childhood. Being brought up by the Claire/Bolingbroke team was pure hell. The tears she wept! The pain, real pain, she learned about so early on, which is why she naturally gravitated toward the pills she found in her mother's medicine cabinet.

Her mother, whose career had been sliding since 1958, due to her various addictions, arrogance and a reputation for being a troublemaker, committed suicide (though it was reported as a car accident) when Joy was only seventeen. Two years later, her father died in a hotel-room fire (also probably suicide). His meager life insurance and savings went toward the education of her younger brothers and sister. Joy had to drop out of Vassar when she was only a freshman, take a job that paid only $50 a week and share a tiny apartment in Greenwich Village with a vile, gum-chewing girl whose name she got through a roommate agency.

She never bought any clothes and some days went without anything to eat except candy bars. More tragic: her childhood had severely impaired her mental and emotional development.

If this material doesn't get to you, she moves quickly to some grisly specific which has you staring at her bug-eyed, all your attention focused on her soft, winsome face as she tells you that her mother, the renowned Maddy Bolingbroke, whose Mrs. Windemere and Hedda Gabler were the greatest ever to be played by an American-trained actress on the New York stage, was obsessed by elimination.

Thus, it was imperative that Joy have her colon cleaned out regularly by a sort of nurse, who came to the house with an enema bag in a black vinyl satchel.

Once a week, this woman, who looked like a witch, took Joy into the bathroom alone and made her lean over while, with a light, feathery touch, she drew small, soft circles around Joy's baby anus, telling her to relax, relax, then plunged the vaseline-soaked nozzle of the enema tube into little Joy.

Terrible pain, screams and kicking while this she-devil held her down and prevented her from reaching the beloved toilet for five full torturous minutes. And then, relief, as Joy sat on the toilet, pushing obediently and eliminating all the week's waste while the woman fondled her breasts and massaged her baby clitoris.

"So that's why I've always preferred it in the ass," Joy said flatly. "Could you pass the cream?"

I reached for the cream pitcher, unable to utter a word, my head dancing with pornographic images.

But more than anything, I was filled with admiration for her openness. How could she admit to all this? I wondered. I had never met anyone who revealed so many hideous things about her life with so little embarrassment.

I, for instance, never told anyone anything that reflected badly on me or my family. My parents' various fights were shameful secrets and were always carried on after the windows were shut so the neighbors wouldn't hear them. It was understood by my brother, sister and me that certain family scandals, like my grandmother's addiction to painkillers and my uncle's frequent bankruptcies in Kansas, were never to be divulged. And never was anyone outside the family to know about my father's emotional frailty and crippling descents into depression.

When my father, who was once an excellent contract lawyer, had a nervous breakdown in his late forties and was asked to resign as a partner from his law firm, the rest of my mother's life was devoted to hiding their diminished wealth from Saint Louis society. Thus, we never moved out of our six-bedroom house on Elm Street in Webster Groves, and my mother continued to have a maid and was adamant that my sister and I see an opera in Chicago at least once a year and make debuts. But our house was never heated above 62 degrees Fahrenheit, our coming-out parties were teas and we saw Madame Butterfly and Tosca commit suicide from the last rows of the second balcony. Even the maid had an extra job she went to in the mornings.

We never questioned the necessity of keeping up a front of financial stability, familial harmony and untroubled emotional life for our friends, neighbors and even first cousins. It wasn't all a facade, however. In truth, things like sexual perversion and criminal acts didn't enter our lives. They resided outside, somewhere in novels and scandal sheets. Though evil had certainly penetrated my daydreams (What if my parents and siblings died in a plane accident and I got all the insurance? What if I asked my brother to demonstrate how men made love? What if I ran away to Forty-second Street and became a hooker?), my parents never gave any indication that such things existed in *their* daydreams and even if they did, they'd long since made it clear that what went on in your head didn't count. What counted was how you *looked* like you thought.

But here, sitting before me, was this fascinating new friend who confessed to loving buggery, gang bangs and drugs and was closer to the craziness of life than anyone I'd ever known. And she was telling it all to me, an outsider. How could she take such a risk?

"How come you trust me not to repeat all this?" I asked one Saturday afternoon in the summer of '69.

It was a landmark day in our friendship, for we had finally progressed from meeting at the lunch counter to seeing each other on weekends. Because it was a beautiful, blue-sky day, we had decided to walk through Central Park, a far more benign place in those days, and splurge on a lunch at the Tavern on the Green. It was still a comfortable, sloppily run beer garden then, not the jungle of chandeliers and mirrors for tourists it later became. We were sitting outdoors on the cement terrace under a musty umbrella eating knockwurst.

"I don't know why, I just trust you," she said sweetly. "You have a sort of midwestern beauty and cleanness and loyalty about your way of thinking. I know you'd never want to hurt me."

I shimmered and blushed with pride over my wonderfulness (though I would have been happier if the "midwestern" had been edited out), and in an attempt to emulate her incredible verbal generosity, said, "You're really brave to admit all you've been through. Some people could really be shocked."

"Well, I'm not ashamed of anything I've done. I hate secrets. I believe the truth, even when it's shocking, should always be told."

I was even more enraptured—if that was possible—by her stand on truth and sighed with compassion for myself, who had had such an uneventful life, who had nothing but a few violent daydreams to my credit. "The thing is, you, yourself, are as interesting as your life is."

She nodded in agreement. She knew she was interesting.

"You know, you really ought to write a book about yourself," I continued.

She lowered her head as her enormous, dusty-gold eyes filled with tears, her nose reddened and her beautiful hands formed themselves into two tight fists.

Why was she looking so miserable?

Because the final prong of her attack had just begun and I was about to be enlisted in her army of personal aides who would help fill the bottomless pit of needs she carted around from party to party, coffee shop to coffee shop, through subways and airplanes and whatever chair, booth or bed she beached on.

But I had no way of knowing that. All I knew was that this dear, darling friend of mine, with her childlike ways and wounded innocence, must not cry. She had suffered enough.

"What's wrong, Joy? Oh, I hope I haven't said anything to offend you."

She reached across the table and clutched my hand piteously. Eyes squeezed shut like a child's, she swung her head back and forth. Fat drops of tears flew through the sunny air.

"I'm so sorry. I thought saying you should write a book was a compliment."

"It—it—is," she said, bowing her head and gasping, not for air, but to stop herself from sobbing and letting the overwhelming, black, horrific sorrow living inside her to escape. "I w-w-want to write. But I can't. I can't concentrate. In the office I have to work. If I even write a letter when I'm at the desk, the office manager starts yelling at me. And I'm so bored just sitting there saying good morning and good afternoon all day."

She had, it turned out, wanted to be a writer ever since she was a little girl and wrote her first letters home from camp, where she had had her first lesbian encounter and then been cruelly—what else?—rejected and disgraced by the camp. Her parents had always encouraged her to write. In fact, that was why she had chosen to work in a publishing firm: to get to know real writers and editors.

But she didn't own a typewriter and it was impossible to concentrate in her apartment because her sleazy roommate played her stereo so loudly and every man she'd ever met told her she had no talent. Even her current boyfriend, Geoffrey Castleman, made fun of her writing.

I was overcome with emotion. To discover that this strange, unusual friend of mine actually had a desire—had the courage and ambition—to record her scandalous tales in a book which she would try to get published was a fantastic revelation. I'd known only one person who wanted to write a whole book—an ethereal classmate of mine with a long neck and practically no shoulders who turned into a manic-depressive after she had her first baby.

But here, sharing her sorrows with me, was the daughter of the renowned Claire-Bolingbroke acting team, someone with grade-A artistic blood coursing through her veins, who had true stories to tell and, to judge from the way she kept me on the edge of my chair as she recounted them, a fabulous talent for narrative.

I was thrilled for her (and for myself, for just *knowing* her) but also indignant. How could this vulnerable, precious talent be stifled by noise, the lack of a typewriter and a cruel boss? How dare her boyfriend denigrate her ability and impede the flow of grotesque information she was willing to impart to the world?

"Something must be done," I said, slicing the air with the side of my hand in the manner of a determined, supracapable woman, which I had adopted since coming to New York. "You need help."

"Oh, nothing will work. I've tried. I still try. But you have no idea. I sit down to write—you know, in longhand—and my roommate turns on her hi-fi. She keeps playing the same Tijuana Brass record over and over. . . ."

"Just tell her to turn it off."

"I can't. And anyhow, with no typewriter . . ."

My chest swelled with anger and resolve. "I'll find a way. You've got to write this book. It's criminal that you're being prevented from doing so."

She tightened her lips to prevent any further sobs from slipping through. "It's no use, Madeleine." Her body slumped forward onto the table. More tears plopped on the place mat.

"Please, Joy, listen to me," I implored. "There must be something I can do. I'd give anything if you'd let me help you."

Thus it was that I "borrowed" a typewriter from the copy department of my advertising agency. It was easy. I took it out of the building in a suitcase I brought in one Friday, saying I was spending the weekend in the Hamptons. (At first Joy was going to steal one of the typewriters from her own office, but there were problems, so many problems. The typewriters were too heavy, and "I don't know," she said mournfully, self-hatingly, "I've just never been able to pull off that kind of thing without looking scared and getting caught.")

I then arranged for her to come to my walk-up apartment on East Twenty-fifth Street every Saturday so she could write alone and in total quiet for long, uninterrupted stretches of time. After making a pot of coffee for her, I would go out around ten A.M. and leave her sitting at my Formica-topped desk, smiling coquettishly, beautiful white hands poised on the keys of the stolen typewriter, eyes gazing dreamily down at the street through my dusty, polyester "glass" curtains.

I would wander around New York until five, visiting friends, going to the movies, shopping or just sitting on a patch of grass in Central Park amid the ice-cream bar wrappers and cigarette butts, reading old magazines.

When I returned home, she would show me a sheaf of papers she had typed and, dewy-eyed with artistic fulfillment, she would give me a bunch of flowers, a Cadbury's chocolate bar or some other imported candy she had bought during her fifteen-minute break at noon. Kissing me good-bye, saying over and over again how grateful she was, she would leave to return to her music-infested apartment to get dressed to go out to one of the many parties she attended with Geoffrey Castleman. Parties to which I was never invited.

It went without saying, it was understood, that someone of my, well, background and standing just never would be. I may have had a small talent for drawing, which was better than being a bookkeeper or a dental assistant, but that was hardly enough to qualify for easy entrance into the bad, bright world she and her boyfriend traveled in.

My role was to help Joy. Period.

This Saturday routine could have conceivably gone on for years (though I like to think I would have rebelled when winter came) if she hadn't become pregnant in early September. She decided to marry Geoffrey in spite of what she called his "definite mean streak."

He was also born in New Jersey, the son of a theatrical agent and as well connected as she through his father, though as far as I could make out, he had failed at every attempt to find work. I met him when he came to pick up Joy at my apartment one Saturday evening. He was a good-looking spoiled brat with extraordinarily well-developed biceps and pectorals bulging under his Italian black leather jacket.

When Joy introduced us, he barely acknowledged me, just kept looking through the window at his Harley Davidson, which he had parked outside. He was justifiably anxious. A group of the multiracial urchins who tormented my street had gathered round to gape at it, touch it and (I hoped) remove whatever loose part they could get their mitts on.

When I offered him tea, he made a graphic gesture indicating that the very thought of tea made him want to throw up and ordered Joy to hurry up. Shuddering with lust brought on by his command, she excitedly gathered her papers together.

She sent me a plaintive, apologetic look for his rudeness as he shoved her arms into her coat and bundled her out the door, glowering at me as if I were a zookeeper who had stolen his favorite animal.

Their wedding was a small family affair, paid for by the Castleman family, for a hundred of his friends, not her friends, she swore, when she explained why she couldn't invite me.

After the wedding, they moved to New Mexico, where he had found a job importing pre-Columbian art from Mexico and, she hinted, maybe a little marijuana on the side.

I sneaked the typewriter back into my ad agency and got on with my life.

It wasn't until 1976, seven years later, that a mimeographed letter, addressed to my old advertising agency, was forwarded to me.

"Dear beautiful, wonderful friends," it said. "I've just written a novel, *The Lost and the Mad*. It's really awful, but my editor says it's great and people will love it. I hope so. It's coming out in November and I wish I could send you all a free copy. Maybe you can get it in the library or something. I'd be eternally grateful if you'd tell your friends about it and kind of suggest they buy a copy. We could use the royalties. Am still ecstatically happy living in Taos with gorgeous Geoffrey. Though I wish he weren't traveling so much in Mexico. I miss New York and my friends more than I can ever say. Hugs, love and kisses to you all. Joy."

Below her signature was a drawing of a little face which at first I thought might be the baby she had been pregnant with, but closer inspection with a magnifying glass showed that it was a good caricature of Joy. There were even two little specks under the eyes which looked like tears.

THREE

I did as the letter instructed: bought the book, found it fascinating and told my friends to buy it. I also wrote her a long letter in care of her publisher, filling her in on all the changes in my own life.

I had come up in the world since I had known her. Shortly after she had left for New Mexico, I met and married Ralph Tyson. He was, like my father, a lawyer, but unlike him in every other way. To begin with, he was a New Yorker, educated at Princeton, even-tempered and emotionally stable. And since the conventions of the times suited him very well, he unthinkingly approved of them all. He was my age, tall and good-looking in a stiff-jawed way. His only physical flaw was his nearsightedness, but because his large, expensive, horn-rimmed glasses suited his face perfectly, he was able to turn even this disadvantage into an asset. He was, to quote my mother to my father behind a door I happened to be standing on the other side of, "the best Madeleine could possibly do."

She adored him and was mortified that they could afford to give me a wedding with only champagne and hors d'oeuvres under a tent on the lawn and not a sit-down dinner with music and dancing.

Ralph's firm specialized in the music industry and he handled several famous concert artists and opera stars. Through him, I gained even more knowledge of celebrities' addictions, sexual deviations, operations, chronic insecurity and financial misdemeanors. I also learned that these world-famous high-achievers could be disciplined and possess a good sense of humor and an uncommon ability to work long hours. Some were even happily married. Knowing all this and hearing Ralph discuss them in his matter-of-fact way robbed their sins—and them—of all the glamour and ghoulish titillation Joy had been so good at provoking.

Thus, I was far less impressed than I had once been by the intimate knowledge of the scandalous behavior of the stars presented in her novel, but what kept my eyes nailed to the page, even as it appalled me, was Joy's weird acceptance of the indignities inflicted upon the heroine, which, like everyone else, I assumed were based on Joy's own experiences.

How can she write such things about herself? I marveled to Ralph, who had started the book and managed to put it down after reading fifty pages. Whatever her magic, it didn't do to him what it did to me. I now realize that magic was much the same as that which she'd exercised over me in the coffee shop so many years before. She made me feel superior. Only then, I felt superior to the depraved celebrities she described. Now, my disdain was directed at Joy and her martyred heroine. For all its faults, *The Lost and the Mad* validated my tenuously held opinion that I had more self-respect and was more liberated than Joy. In other words, the book lowered, rather than raised, my consciousness.

Whereas my husband didn't need a book to make him feel superior. He already knew he was. Perhaps to all women. But that's another story.

In most ways, I considered myself fortunate to have found

Ralph Tyson, have two children by him and live in a sunny, high-ceilinged brownstone apartment between Fifth and Sixth avenues on West Eleventh Street.

In those early years, I was immersed in my children, Roberta and Harold, and, having left my advertising job during my first pregnancy, in my painting. For I had not lost my ambition to paint. Every day, I stole a couple of hours in front of a canvas I set up in the little maid's room I'd converted into a studio in the back of our apartment. I didn't know where my drawing would lead, but I was fascinated enough by my work to keep at it and not live vicariously through Ralph. Like the glorious Marisa (though minus her staff of servants) I gradually, rather painlessly, when I compare my experience to that of other women, came to see that I needed more fulfillment than that which motherhood and wifehood provided.

And so, in between shopping, taking the children to the park, feeding them and cleaning the apartment, I painted my fruits and flowers and the occasional insect. Insects always interested me. Perhaps because, like us, they live as part of a uniform mass. Perhaps because I think we could learn something awful from them. Something which apes and wolves and birds have failed to tell us.

But I was still a long way from finding it. I supposed I was "blocked," but I barely knew what that meant in those days. What I did know, all too clearly, was that, although my painstaking, formalized skills were definitely improving, my work was still not good enough. Though talented, I still had a lot more developing to do—emotionally and technically—before any original inspirations would start leaping off my paintbrush onto my tidily stretched two-by-two-foot canvases.

A whole year passed before Joy acknowledged my letter and called me. She was dying to see me, she said breathlessly. She had been meaning to call for months, but had been up to her ears in "God, all kinds of shit." But she was longing to talk to me. She *missed* me. She had never forgotten all I'd done for her that summer, back in 1969, the happiest summer in her life, when we'd known each other. Would I like to have lunch at the Sign of the Dove?

Yes, yes, I trilled. I was ecstatic at the thought of seeing her. The children were wrangling over the cereal box which had just spilled—along with the milk—the TV was blaring the Mickey Mouse song and Ralph had just told me we couldn't afford to take a skiing vacation in Vermont, which was, I yelled as he was leaving for his ten-hour workday, a fucking lie.

After I had wiped down the kids, the table and the floor and loaded the dishwasher, it occurred to me that that summer I'd spent wandering around New York on Saturdays and bent over a drawing board in my cubicle Monday through Friday might have been the happiest summer of my life too.

I desperately wanted to giggle and gossip with Joy and relive those gay, formless times.

I was also curious to see if she had been changed by her new life, which, I had learned from an article about her in *People,* was radically different from the one she had been leading when I knew her.

For now, not only was she rich, she was also thin. The full-page photo of her, under the headline DAUGHTER OF THE THEATER HONES MEMORIES AND BRINGS HOME BIG BUCKS, showed an almost anorexic Joy. The hollows in her cheeks gave her face drama and shape. Beside her sat Geoffrey, plumper and far less menacing than he had formerly appeared to be. But not a word about a child. Just fans. Another picture showed her sitting before a foot-high stack of mail allegedly from readers who swore their lives and minds had been improved by reading *The Lost and the Mad.*

I expected a whole new skinny human being to greet me

when I arrived at the Sign of the Dove, but it was not to be.

Standing near one of the floral arrangements the restaurant was famous for, little nose buried in a cluster of chrysanthemums she had whimsically decided to sniff just as I was coming through the foyer, was the same, the identical, Joy I'd known seven years before: still about eight pounds overweight, still with wispy blond curls hovering around her soft-edged face and the same half-open trembling mouth.

"Hi, Madeleine," she said. Solemnly, almost reverently, she threw her arms around me and gave me a suffocating, long-lasting, breast-to-breast hug that was the basis for my subsequent suspicions that, when all was said and done, women were probably higher than men on her list of sexual diversions.

As we walked into the dining room, its beauty took my breath away. With its graceful archways, bare brick walls and giant urns, it could have been a set for Violetta's country house in *La Traviata*. How paradoxical, I remember thinking, that Joy would invite me to such an elegant, flower-filled restaurant, so unlike the sordid places—the Beverly Hills bedroom with its chains and plastic decor, the policeman's urinal, the grubby airports—described in the novel that had made her fortune.

"Your table is ready, Mrs. Castleman," murmured the maître d'. He was dark and short, with a well-oiled toupee that sat squarely on his low forehead. The tone and the bow that followed his words were sexual, that of a man who had been well rewarded for the respect and attention he accorded her.

She gave him a chummy, teasing grin. "Thanks, Mario. This is one of my oldest friends. Mrs. . . . ."

"Madeleine Tyson," I said, extending my hand.

"Delighted to meet you." He bowed again, though hardly with the same fervor.

He was a thug and sleeping with Joy. I felt it with every bone in my body, but can offer no proof of this since I never saw him again, nor did she ever mention him later.

He led us to what was apparently "her" table. It was near the front where we could see everyone who left or entered the restaurant. To have such a table, I'd learned through Ralph, was a common ploy of agents and small-potatoes producers on the lookout for anything with power or money which might walk in. Joy, a successful, acclaimed writer, should not have had to be aware of such a stratagem, much less use it. But the fact that she was and did was fitting.

"You use your husband's name?" she asked after we were seated.

"Yes." For a time I had thought of keeping my maiden name, but both Ralph and I had decided Gibbons was too ordinary and made people think of monkeys, whereas Tyson was the name of the tragic but illustrious family in *A Long Day's Journey into Night*.

She nodded approvingly. "Women who keep their maiden names are fools."

A waiter flicked a giant white napkin into my lap and I grinned at Joy. "What a change from the coffee shop counters," I said gleefully.

She smiled compassionately at my naive enjoyment and allowed her eyes to wander over to the next table, where a couple was being seated. She stared at them unabashedly. The man looked like Oleg Cassini, but wasn't. His partner was a young girl whose gigantic breasts were giving her early widow's hump. Not even the two feet of swirling white-blond hair trailing across her back could conceal it.

"I was riveted by your book," I said, trying to bring her attention back to our table. "You've got to tell me what parts were autobiographical. Did you actually do any of those things your heroine did?"

Slowly, as if coming out of a trance, she returned her eyes to me. "No. Maybe. Oh God. In a way. I don't know."

I pryed no further, realizing that, like many of Ralph's clients, she was unsure of what biographical data should be revealed to her public. She was still in the process of building a legend about herself which hadn't quite jelled in her mind.

It would never jell. She would always be shifting the facts, moving a date here, and rearranging the terms of a relationship there, like a court painter working on a vast, multipeopled canvas which never quite satisfied.

But neither she nor I knew that then. In my mind, she was well on her way to building a great masochistic legend as solid and heart rending as Marilyn Monroe's.

"So tell me about the present. What's been happening to you? There's no mention of your child in the article in *People*."

"I had a miscarriage. Three of them, actually. I keep trying, but no luck."

"How sad. I'm so sorry."

"The only good thing was that each time I miscarried, I lost weight. That's why I was so skinny in the photographs in *People*. But I always gain it back."

"Do you know why you miscarry?"

"Yes. Because of an abortion my mother made me have when I was sixteen. If I hadn't had it, I'd have a family now." Fists clenched. Ferocious little will being thwarted. No, she hadn't changed at all. "It was a vile, back-street abortion. Someday, I'll write about it, but it's still too horrible to even think about."

"So tell me about the present," I said gently. "Do you still live in New Mexico?"

Her eyes flickered over to the June-December couple, then returned to mine. "I've just rented a seven-room furnished apartment on Riverside Drive and Eighty-eighth Street with money from the book."

"How great! With a view of the river?" I asked, trying to keep the envy out of my voice. To have earned enough money from one's own art to rent a huge apartment on the river seemed to be the most blessed thing that could happen to a woman.

"I shouldn't have taken it. I can't afford it and it's too big really just for me alone."

"Aren't you still married to Geoffrey?"

"I don't know. I think so."

"What do you mean?"

"Well, he's kind of disappeared."

"How awful. When?"

"When the book came out. His ego couldn't take it. The last I heard he was living with some teenager in California."

I was longing to know if it was he who had tied her to the bedpost and sodomized her and made her carry drugs through airports, but she was looking at the menu, chatting about the food and recommending the Scotch smoked salmon and several other pricey dishes in this already pricey restaurant. I was aghast. When I went to such a place, I headed straight for the egg dishes and salads. It was an automatic reflex instilled during my family's four-flushing years that Ralph, not surprisingly, found very endearing.

But Joy would have none of this penny-pinching. If I insisted upon having an omelette, it would have to be stuffed with beluga caviar, and the only salad I could consider was the crab and avocado. And so I had both.

It was toward dessert (profiteroles with chocolate sauce) that we began talking about money. She had made a lot, over a million dollars, she said. (When I later told this to Ralph, he guffawed: "No way." He was probably right. In the seventies, no author made a million on a first novel.) In any event, the amount she quoted was of no significance for, in one year, she was practically broke. She had spent it all on her siblings, who were still wretched, and on Geoffrey Castleman, who was even more wretched. All she had done for herself was buy a few clothes and rent the ridiculously expensive apartment on Riverside Drive, which, if she didn't write a new book fast, she'd have to vacate within a year.

I believe, even today, she was telling the truth about giving the money away. Though her greatest talent consists in manipulating money and services out of people more privileged than she, she has always been generous toward those whom she deems to be truly miserable. I could possibly consider this Robin Hood aspect of her character appealing, were it not for the fact that she has consistently viewed me as one of the people, ripe for plundering, traveling through her personal Sherwood Forest.

"I have just enough money to tide me over for a year . . . as long as Geoffrey doesn't come after me demanding more cash."

"But he has deserted you. He has no right to claim money from you," I said indignantly.

"He says he helped me write the book and should be compensated. But he didn't, you know. My editor did. Oh God, Madeleine, he was so wonderful. An Englishman. His accent alone would make you want to go to bed with him."

There followed a long description of her editor, Nigel Benson-Smith, a married, Oxford-educated former poet who had tumbled from his ivory tower at Langford Press into a passionate relationship with her that included doing "semi-perverse, kind-of-outrageous" things on the desk in his office and in the front seat of his adorable two-door Jaguar. "I never could have done the book without his help. I came all the way from Taos and stayed with my sister in New York while Nigel did the editing. I'd bring in pages and he'd kind of rearrange them and make them work," she said with a mischievous smile that managed to include both me and the Oleg Cassini character, who had finally noticed her. "He has such a brilliant, elegant mind."

"Is he going to help you with your next book?" I asked.

"Well, no. He's busy with something else." And: "We kind of stopped seeing each other. Our affair just ran its course, if you know what I mean. It was inevitable."

I inclined my head knowingly, but I didn't know at all what she meant, never having screwed an editor and gotten a bestseller out of it.

"The awful thing is that Geoffrey found out about Nigel and me and beat me up. He almost broke my arm." Stoically now. As if brutality were a natural part of life. "I *liked* Nigel, but I really *love* Geoffrey still. But I know that he doesn't love me. All he wants is the little money I have left."

I reacted as I'd always reacted: with rage at the cruel people and cruel circumstances surrounding her fragile, star-crossed being and an overwhelming, almost compulsive, desire to right her wrongs and reestablish justice.

"You love someone who nearly broke your arm? How could you?"

"I keep hoping he'll change."

"But even if he did change, how could you forget what he did?"

"It's all the drugs he took when he was in high school. He can't help it."

"Of course he can."

"The last time I saw him, three months ago, I let him come over to see me in the apartment and made dinner for him and after he'd had only two drinks, he forced me into the bedroom and kind of raped me. I was so scared I wrote out a check for ten thousand dollars to get rid of him. I know what he'll do with it. He'll buy some stuff and, you know, get started selling again."

Buy what? I wanted to ask, but thought better of it. I didn't really want to know if it was grass, heroin or encyclopedias. I didn't want to know anything about this rapist drug-running, good-for-nothing monster who continued to screw and exploit my friend.

"I'm just afraid he'll come back," she said, eyes down, head lowered as her little claw closed over the check. "It's on me," she whispered piteously and began a five-minute search through her voluminous satchel for her credit card, which she just knew was there.

I thought about offering to pay the check myself, but decided that, after all, she had invited me and anyhow, I didn't have enough money with me. (Ralph kept me on a rather tight rope.) In any case, I was already contemplating a far greater gift for her.

The waiter pounced on her credit card as soon as she put it on the table, which made me wonder if there had been other times when she had managed to forget her card and made them give her credit. For all the maître d's attentiveness, I doubted that free meals were included in his services.

"What I want is to make a clean break with Geoffrey. I've just got to forget that I'm in love with him. He'll end up taking all my money away if I don't. He's already gotten over half of it. Do you think I should give it all to him?"

"No, for God's sake," I practically screeched. "You need a lawyer. Fast."

"I can't afford a lawyer, Madeleine. I've just got to work this thing out myself."

"But you'll never be able to work it out if he keeps threatening you and you keep dreaming you are still in love with him."

"Sure I can." Bravely, but face about to disintegrate. Her lower lip was trembling so hard it looked like it was going to fall off.

"You need someone mean and strong to fight this for you."

"But who? Where can I . . . ?"

"I'll talk to Ralph."

"Why? Does he know about law?"

"He's a lawyer. Don't you remember my letter when I wrote and told you I'd done the sensible thing and married a lawyer like my father?"

"Oh yes, but I forgot." Her face broke into a gentle, tragic smile. "All I remembered was that you had two children and thinking how much I wished I had children. Tell me, do you love your kids a lot?"

"They're great. They really are. I can't believe how much I love them. And I want you to meet them when you meet Ralph."

"Are you bringing them up as Catholics?" She had not been brought up in any religion and had always been dreamily fascinated by Catholicism. A lot of masochists are.

"No, I've definitely given it up."

"How could you?"

"Because I don't believe a word of it. It's a macho, desert religion invented by wandering, desperate people who love authority. Nietzsche was right when he said it was a slaves' religion. And I can't stand the fact that someone as dreary and passive as Mary is the main woman they glorify."

"I love Mary. She's so beautiful . . . all those madonnas. She suffered so much."

"I infinitely prefer any of the beautiful, powerful goddesses from ancient times over Mary. I wish we could bring back all of them. I even love their names. Isis, Astarte, Aphrodite, Diana."

Her eyes shifted lazily toward the couple sitting near us, but once started on religion, I didn't shut up that easily. "Isis or Diana could do more for women's dignity than a million equal-opportunity laws. I've already given Roberta and Harold a picture book about ancient myths so they'll get started on the right foot."

"Mary is more real. When you've been through what I've been through, you'll see."

"I'm never going to go through what you've been through. I can't afford to with two kids to bring up."

"I'd love to meet them."

"You will, but first of all I want you to talk to Ralph."

"You're so lucky to have a decent husband. I'm so happy for you, Madeleine. I always knew you'd make the right move, marry a good man. I think you're terrific and someday you're going to be a famous, really respected artist. I just know it."

"What I've been thinking is that there's a chance I can get Ralph to help you with a divorce," I said, ignoring the compliment, but enjoying it just the same. "He wouldn't charge much. Maybe nothing at all, if we present the problem to him correctly."

"Oh, he wouldn't. I couldn't—He doesn't even know me."

"We can try."

"He won't like me."

"Of course he will."

"God, I'd be so grateful. But don't please, don't do anything if it will, you know, get you into trouble."

"What do you mean? You talk like he's my boss or something."

"All husbands are bosses."

"Oh shit."

"My mother always said being married is a job."

"But your mother had her own money."

"Not at the end, she didn't."

"Well, I don't work for Ralph." Didn't I? "Look, why don't you come and have dinner with us tonight and tell him all about Geoffrey wanting to get your money away?"

And that was how Joy got her first divorce. Cost to her: the price of a lunch at the Sign of the Dove. Cost to me: one year of wondering, after Joy had met and flattered Ralph until he burbled, whether he was getting paid in semi-perverse, kind-of-outrageous fucks.

FOUR

By the end of that year, Joy had signed a separation agreement with Geoffrey which, thanks to Ralph, stopped him from making any more claims on her money.

I saw Geoffrey only once more before he died. He was waiting for his lawyer, who was already a half hour late, in the silent reception room of Ralph's offices. He had grown stodgy, almost inert, after seven years of imbibing his magic mushrooms—or whatever he did—in New Mexico. It took considerable faith on my part to believe he had recently brutalized Joy, whose mind and wiles had done nothing but sharpen themselves during her exile with him from New York. In fact all traces of his mean streak had vanished. Whatever he had once done to Joy, it was pretty clear that he, not she, had been vanquished and chastized in the end.

He was accompanied by a waif with pimples dancing across her forehead like little pink bugs. Perhaps they were a side effect of the drugs he fed her. If she was eighteen, it was a very young eighteen. Her leggy, emaciated body was covered in a bright, grasshopper-colored pantsuit which added to the bug effect. So did her unusual alertness. She looked as if she expected the police to burst into those sedate, wood-paneled law offices any moment. Her name was Marin, after the county in California.

Remembering this odd pair makes me nostalgic for the sixties and the little trail of malcontents and losers who followed the counter culture into the seventies. I hope she ended up putting on some weight and working in Silicon Valley. I hear a lot of them did.

Geoffrey died rather stupidly one year later, in a fire on Rodeo Drive, while rescuing someone's parrot which had been trained to say "What did the President know and when did he know it?" Joy, who tells the story, does an excellent imitation of the parrot.

During that same year Joy finished the first draft of her second novel, *Fate Kisses Back,* sold it to Manoff Press, one of the hottest publishing houses in New York, and had a torrid affair with her editor, Isabel Swann, a willowy redhead who looked as though she had glided out of a pre-Raphaelite painting. According to a *Time* magazine article about new women editors, Isabel had—in addition to beauty—the ability to carve a bestseller out of any book she touched. The whole of New York publishing was half in love with her, but Joy was the one who nailed her.

Almost every night around 8:30, after I'd fed Ralph and the children, Joy would call me to "check in," as she put it, before she went out with the workaholic Isabel, who didn't leave the office until nine. Joy's phone calls were like delicious, licentious desserts at the end of my responsible, dutiful day.

It was the middle seventies, remember, when the women's movement was in full force and the publishing world had finally woken up to Bloomsbury's commercial potential as a prime escape fantasy for women fed up with a browbeating world. Overnight, it seemed, Vita and Virginia became household names among thinking women and sapphic love was elevated to a glamorous, snobbish level it had never enjoyed before. It was exactly the right time for Joy to have her first publicly acknowledged lesbian affair.

She delivered up so many details about her relationship with the passionately jealous Isabel that I was ashamed of my suspicions about her and Ralph. No one could be having an affair with my husband and simultaneously carry on a relationship as all-consuming as the one she was having with her editor. With their fights on the streets, public hair pullings in all-girl, after-hours bars, their shared amyl nitrate habit and the thousands of vibrator and dildo-induced orgasms, there simply wasn't time for Joy to remunerate Ralph with her body.

I was clamoring to meet the magnificent, notorious Isabel and after waiting some time for Joy to suggest it and getting nowhere, I asked point-blank during one of our evening phone calls for her to introduce me.

"Sure," she said quickly. "Of course. I'll try to fix it up. But, you know, she's difficult. Straight people sort of turn her off."

"I won't say anything dumb. I mean, I'm not a total fool."

"Of course you wouldn't. I don't mean that. But she's, well, critical. As a matter of fact, I've already told her that I want her to meet my lawyer's wife and she said—"

"Lawyer's wife? Is that how you refer to me?"

"Of course not. I said it just to explain who you are."

"I am a painter, who used to be an art director, who's known you for almost eight years."

"I know you're an artist. A marvelous, brilliant painter and I just know you're going to get recognized soon. I've been telling every gallery owner I meet about you and I—"

"I find it perfectly revolting that you refer to me as your lawyer's wife." My voice was rising higher and louder. Ralph could hear me in the next room. "And how can you call him *your* lawyer when you haven't ever paid him?"

Ralph was at the door, eyebrows raised, enjoying himself.

"Listen, you have no idea how grateful I am to you," Joy said. "I really appreciate what you and Ralph have done. I'd be *dead* by now probably if you hadn't . . ."

"I know that. Why do you think I, *I,* got Ralph to help you?"

"I have an idea: Why don't we have tea at Isabel's apartment in the Village? I'd really love you to see it and that way she won't have to come all the way to Riverside Drive."

"Okay," I chirped. I smiled at Ralph. I had gotten what I wanted. Intimidation definitely works with her, I remember thinking. But of course, I was wrong. Intimidation got her to do what you wanted for a millisecond, but she was already planning ways to extract a new favor from you to make up for cornering her.

I was invited to have tea two Thursdays later. At three o'clock, I was to go to Isabel's place on Grove Street, a tiny strip of land off Seventh Avenue adorned with nineteenth-century buildings. It was a damp, chilly October day. I had planned to arrive a nice, uneager fifteen minutes late, but had walked so quickly from West Eleventh Street I was standing in front of her building at five minutes to three. It began to rain, but I trudged around the block twice to use up some time. It also wasn't a bad idea to arrive with disheveled, rained-on hair. It took the edge off my bourgeois appearance. Part of me was still seething over the lawyer's wife epithet, but I was making an effort to force it out of my mind. Didn't I typecast Joy as my "crazy writer friend"? Well, wasn't she doing the same to me?

I rang Isabel's bell at 3:11 and obediently followed her peremptory order to "walk up three flights."

She opened the door just far enough for me to enter. "Joy's not here yet, but come on in."

She was exactly as I expected her to be: hair the color of deep-red autumn leaves, pale skin with a suggestion of former freckles, red-blond eyelashes and one of those wondrous figures without a trace of fat on them which still appear rounded. She was wearing a vaguely Edwardian silk kimono which made me think of Aubrey Beardsley's drawings of proud, long-fingered ladies with vice-ridden little animals underfoot. There were, however, two cigarette burns on Isabel's sash.

I stepped into the tiny foyer—a blur of dark brocade-covered walls with ostrich plumes in a Chinese *sang de boeuf* urn flaring from a corner. "I'm so happy to meet you. Joy's told me so much about you," I said boringly, timidly.

A teakettle whistled. "Oh, there's the water. Just go in the living room and sit down. I'll be right back." She vanished behind a lacquered screen.

The living room was cluttered with velvet-upholstered Victorian furniture. Crammed against a far wall was a shawl-covered baby grand piano littered with books, manuscripts and magazines, on top of which were ashtrays, half-empty wineglasses and things like binoculars, spectacles and a couple of watercolors on miniature easels. A desk in a corner sported the same sort of paraphernalia. Heavily tasseled curtains hung on each side of the windows. A lamp, which should have been a Tiffany lamp, but was plain brass and modern, glowed weakly from a tortuously twisted side table.

I sat down on a curved, stiff-cushioned settee, crossed my legs and ordered myself to relax. But all I could do was remember having read somewhere that everyone is someone's awful friend. Sitting there in this musty, elegant lair of female iniquity, I realized my time had finally come to validate this sour truth with my robust, size-twelve presence.

Isabel returned with a silver tray in her arms. On it were three plain mugs with tea bags in them, some Ritz crackers, a slab of cream cheese and a bottle of red Italian wine. I forced a smile. I had foregone lunch, expecting (from what well of eternally bubbling, midwestern wishful thinking?) that the food accompanying our tea would be as generous and elaborate as high tea in an English novel.

Just as she was putting the tray down, a key turned in the front-door lock and Joy entered.

Isabel greeted her with a sultry, sulky kiss on the cheek. Joy made the error of not kissing her back. She was too jittery and frothy with chatter to pay attention to such details. (As she always was when two of her marks—or helpers, or whatever Isabel and I were—met.) "You're here, Madeleine. Great. Oh, I'm really sorry to be late. I had this cab, God, I don't want to go into it. The rain. Where shall I put my umbrella? Mmmm, Ritz crackers." She couldn't stop talking. "Oh Isabel, you made tea. How adorable! I feel really English. Don't you love this apartment, Madeleine? Isabel, where is chapter five? I can't find it at home." Searching for the missing chapter, she went over to the piano and started picking up ashtrays and dirty wineglasses.

"Don't *touch* those," Isabel said harshly.

Joy backed away from the piano, sending a see-what-I-have-to-go-through look in my direction. I shrank into the sofa, rather hoping that one of their famous hair-pulling scenes would ensue and wondering if Joy would expect me to separate them—as bystanders in movies are wont to do—or if she would want me to just leave.

"Ah, there it is." Joy darted a foreshortened index finger at a thin pile of yellow paper. She looked fearfully at the editor.

Isabel went over to the piano and looked at the yellow sheets. "It isn't here. It's at the office. I've still got a lot of work to do on it." She turned to me and, without changing her tone or manner, said, "Have some tea."

She sat down and picked up one of the mugs. As she leaned forward, the top of her kimono gaped open to reveal an eggshell satin camisole trimmed in lace.

I picked up a mug, saw that the tea had gone a deep mahogany color and looked around for a place to put the tea bag. All the ashtrays were on the piano, which I didn't dare go near. "I love your Victorian furniture," I said as I squeezed the tepid tea bag. "It really goes with the style of the building." I looked admiringly around the room, and slipped the damp tea bag onto the silver tray.

"Not there," Isabel commanded, leaning forward and putting the tea bag on the plate with the Ritz crackers.

"Sorry," I whispered humbly.

"I actually hate this apartment," Isabel said, after acknowledging my apology with a brief nod. "I want to move to the country." She sent Joy a taunting smile.

"Isabel wants to move to Connecticut, but I keep telling her commuting would be perfectly awful," Joy said mournfully, but still combatively.

Isabel's nostrils stiffened. This was clearly an old bone they tussled over.

"It's the drunks and transvestites in this neighborhood—"

"There are plenty of drunks on commuter trains."

"I need air."

"You'll get hay fever in the summertime and in the winter it's so cold your eyelashes freeze."

"Only if you're crying."

Joy sent me another little glance, which I took to mean that if anyone in this relationship was doing the crying it was she, not Isabel.

"I *hate* the country." Joy's fist lightly pounded the stiff velour upholstery of her chair.

"West Eleventh Street sometimes feels like country to me, especially in the spring when the trees are in bloom," I said, taking Joy's side, not because I especially agreed with her (I often dreamed of having a place in the country), but because I'd always defended Joy when I thought she was being persecuted.

Isabel's eyes bulged at me alarmingly, then turned back to Joy. "I want a garden and a sun room and a raccoon going through the garbage. And a big dog," she said firmly.

"You'll be lonely and when you get snowed in, they'll plow your house last," Joy moaned.

I glanced at my watch, picked up two Ritz crackers—I was starving—and shoved them into my mouth. Slowly, fearful of knocking something over on the cluttered table in front of me, I got to my feet. My legs were unsteady.

"Why would they plow my house last?" Isabel asked tensely. "Why do you say that?"

"Because that's the way life is," Joy said with unusual passion for someone whose social performances were normally so controlled. Clearly she wanted her editor to be in town and accessible to her.

I almost wanted to stay, but having risen and made my rejection of them clear, if only to myself—they still hadn't noticed that I was standing—I didn't want to backtrack. "I just realized I have to pick up my son at school. He's not taking the school bus because I have to take him to the dentist," I announced rather loudly.

"Oh Madeleine, we haven't talked to you at all. I'm so sorry . . ." Joy said.

"That's not why—listen, I'm so sorry. Here I thought I was free as a bird this afternoon and remembered just this minute that poor Harold's waiting for me."

"I didn't know you had children," Isabel said. Her voice was neutral, but her eyes were those of a Charcot or the young Freud examining the latest female hysteric to enter his office.

"Yes. Two. A boy and a girl. Listen, thank you for tea. I really enjoyed it."

Isabel rose and extended her hand, all smiles now. "I do wish you could stay."

"Yes. So do I. Do you know where I put my umbrella?"

"You left it outside." The kimono lapped at her ankles as she walked swiftly to the front door and opened it. "It was really sweet of you to come by . . . in all this rain."

Joy was standing beside me. She put her hand on my arm and raised herself on tiptoe to kiss me good-bye, which wasn't really necessary. Though she looks much smaller, I'm actually only about two inches taller than she is. "I'll talk to you tomorrow," she said warmly.

I had stepped out into the hall, but both of them lingered to look at me fondly. It's amazing how leaving can enhance an unwanted guest's position. I almost felt good about myself. "Thank you very much for tea and good luck with chapter five," I said and galloped down the stairs.

When Ralph came home that night I described every detail of my unpleasant afternoon. I was even mean-spirited enough to suggest that he send Joy a bill for his services.

"Waste of time," he said laconically. "She hasn't any money."

"She's got her advance on the second book."

"You really want me to take that away from her?"

"No."

"She's distracted because she's in love."

"How can she be? It's such an angry, bickering relationship."

"It's not worth getting upset over. You shouldn't take it so hard." It was always a little like this with Ralph. If I confided in him that something was difficult for me or that someone had hurt me, his basic response was to tell me to buck up. "She's too busy having a good time with Isabel to think about her old friends."

"Well, they didn't look like they were having a good time talking about the country versus the city."

"If you want to have Joy as a friend, you have to take her on her own terms," he said and returned to whatever he was doing. The crossword puzzle, I think. "She's not exactly run-of-the-mill."

And I thought, for the first time, Even if she isn't interested in him, who's to say he isn't attracted to her?

A cold, sullen rage—a rage worthy of Agnes Moorehead—rose up in my chest, and far away, in some bleak room in my mind, I heard dungeon keys turning in locks. My hands turned cold and I felt as though I were choking.

That night, after the kids were in bed, I told him every nauseating thing Joy had revealed to me about her affair with the mad, dildo-loving Isabel. He laughed heartily and scornfully, as if he were viewing their wars and depraved goings-on from some great, smug anthropological distance and was thoroughly repulsed.

But he wasn't. All he wanted was to get into bed with the two of them. And eventually did.

It was Isabel who informed me of this. "I want Ralph Tyson out of my bedroom *now*" was how she put it to me one winter morning at seven A.M. when she phoned. I had thought Ralph was in Chicago, but apparently he was eight blocks away and had been depositing his seed into the two of them all through the night.

When Ralph came home two hours later, I started screaming. The kids had left for school on the school bus and there was nothing to stop me as I emptied myself of my anger and frustration. I cried, pounded the walls, tore at his clothes, flung open the windows and roared. It was wonderful. I love anger. I love the way it clarifies your feelings and expands you, so unlike fear, which stays inside, slyly contracting you.

And what I felt that morning was that I no longer wanted to serve this son of a bitch who had betrayed me. For I did serve him. Joy's mother was right. Marriage was a job and he became my boss the day I opted to quit my job and stay home with the children.

In the beginning, I had accepted the loss of pride such an arrangement entailed. My mother had served my father, too.

Nevertheless, because she had a maid, her services were less direct. A maid is a kind of buffer that makes the whole process less demeaning. Plus she has a salary, which I did not. Plus she doesn't have to sleep with her employer. I don't know if I thought all these things through while I was screaming, but I certainly thought them later.

He tried to calm me, but pretty soon he was shouting too. We bellowed back and forth for half an hour or so until we both started crying. Wiping his tears, he mournfully explained how the night he spent with them—the *only* night, he swore—was not his fault. He was so overworked and tense at the office, he had lost all control; Joy and Isabel, who had set out to prey on his weakness, had tricked and seduced him.

In the end, I forgave him. To get back some of my self-respect, I had an affair with a pot-smoking artist I'd met at a gallery opening. I learned a few new snaky copulatory movements, and somehow Ralph and I survived that first set of infidelities, but the marriage was essentially over. Two years later, we divorced.

I realize my description of Ralph is rather shadowy. This is partly because I'm writing about Joy and not Ralph and me, but also because the man I knew during our ten years of marriage is vague and insubstantial in my own memory. He has long since been replaced by the stolid, former-husband figure, now married to one of his firm's paralegals, who takes Roberta and Harold to Maine every summer, counsels me on investments and pays child support with a regularity Joy's mother would have envied.

To visualize this hardworking, responsible, missionary-position-loving person carousing with Isabel and Joy and their vibrators defeats my imagination.

The main things I learned from the experience were that my kind of midwestern loyalty and clean outlook, which Joy had once praised so lavishly, was not very useful and that you never know, even after years of marriage, what kinky things your husband—no matter how conventional he appears to be—really wants to do in bed. Which is exactly what prostitutes have been trying to tell us all along.

In addition, I learned that Joy's endless recitals of degradation and perversity could provoke two entirely different reactions from her audiences, both of which were profitable to her. Either you felt superior to her, as I did, and therefore happy to give her whatever she wanted. Or her perversity excited your lust, as it did Ralph's, and you were therefore willing to do what she asked, provided you could also screw her.

She never lost. And she always had fun.

I dropped her, of course. Though she left several messages with our answering service, I refused to return her calls. I suppose I could have confronted her, but I knew that she would deny being the seducer and turn the facts around to show that somehow she had been Isabel's and Ralph's victim. That she had never *meant* for what had happened to happen. That she still wanted to be my friend, or, rather, still wanted me in her stable of people who did favors for her. I simply did not want to go through that.

The removal of my friendship had little effect on her career. With Isabel's considerable help, she produced *Fate Kisses Back,* a graphic account of the pernicious, gang-raping, drug-taking playmates who used to visit her family's mansion in the horse country of north central New Jersey, which had grown six extra bedrooms and retained two more servants than it had had when she first described it to me in the coffee shop.

The increased opacity of the prose attracted more praise from the critics than the first book, but it sold less well and failed to make the bestseller list. Nevertheless, it established her as a "brand name" in the publishing business. It was impossible not to keep track of her.

An article in *The Village Voice* compared her work to that of Joan Didion, Margaret Drabble and Jill Robinson. Though the author (male) of the article did not consider her as talented as any of the above, he declared that Joy Castleman "described the tragic, contemporary feminine dilemma" better than all of them.

When her divorce from Geoffrey Castleman became final, she managed to be present at every party *Women's Wear Daily* found worth mentioning and was often a guest on local talk shows, where she was introduced as a "literary personality" or, more accurately, a "hot property."

Her circle of admirers, fans and personal helpers was so vast that every few years our paths would cross and I would run into someone who knew her who would tell me how charming, funny and fascinating she was and how he or she was going to help her find a new editor, a new agent, lend her their summer house, type a manuscript for her or whatever.

Sometimes I tried to warn them that they were being used, but they were so completely under her spell they wouldn't listen and were even suspicious of my interference.

"Joy always speaks well of you," Mary Farrar, her new literary agent, said coldly when I hinted at how treacherous Joy could be. Mary and I had met through our daughters, who went to school together, and we had become rather good friends before I spoke ill of her darling new client.

Poor disheveled Mary. She was the perfect mark for Joy. She was no more than thirty-five, but already had jowls and always looked as though she was just emerging from a Bloomingdale's after-Christmas sale. She was one of those exhausted, has-everything women: a husband, two children, a fifty-hour-a-week job, a cat, a dog, a huge rent-controlled

apartment and commitments to friends and women's orga-
nizations all over the city. Her vice was mothering and it was
destroying her mind and body faster than any mind-changing
drug.

How could Joy resist her? How could Mary not succumb?
I saw what was happening, but there was nothing I could do.
After I heard Joy was moving into Mary's apartment to write
her third novel, I again tried to caution her when I saw her
at a school parents' meeting. She listened to what I had to
say, then turned her head away as if she couldn't bear the
sight of me.

It's possible Joy told her of her affair with Ralph and she
assumed my warnings stemmed from some deep-seated, long-
ago sour grapes. Though not a celebrity, Ralph was a distin-
guished lawyer and worth bragging about. He was also male
and the more male lovers Joy mentioned, the more she kept
up her reputation as a bisexual, which, as the decade wore
on, became more marketable than straight lesbianism.

And so I learned to keep silent when people spoke of Joy.
I let them experience for themselves the betrayal which I
knew would follow. A few sought me out later to list their
grievances.

Her second husband, Frederick Worth, was one of those
who came to me for consolation. Ralph had briefly represented him in the early seventies, so I'd known him before
he met Joy. Though possessed of a weak chin and a long,
rabbity-cheeked face, he had been a promising musical com-
edy star before he married Joy. After she divorced him, he
invited himself to dinner at my apartment several times to
lament over her ruthless treatment of him. In their brief two-
year marriage, he had ruined his career and lost all his savings
by insisting on acting in and producing an off-Broadway musical based on *Fate Kisses Back*. And though he didn't mention
it, it was apparent from his reddened, sniffly nose and twitchy

movements that he was also doing a lot of cocaine. I'm not sure where he is now or what he's doing. All I know is he never starred in anything again.

A typist who had once worked in Ralph's office who never got paid for typing the manuscript of Joy's third novel called me at least five times. She was so stunned by Joy's offhand treatment of her she had talked herself into thinking that I, the cuckold, would make good Joy's debt.

Even a TV talk show host who lent Joy money to buy several designer dresses to wear on his show called to complain that Joy had never paid him back, claiming the clothes were a gift. Tribute, actually.

One person who never turned to me for sympathy was Isabel Swann, though, like everyone else, she too was eventually discarded by Joy when something better came along— in this case, a new publisher with a more generous and effective promotion department.

Isabel's career wasn't damaged in any way by Joy's defection. I understand that she's currently in line to become the president of a media conglomerate which has its headquarters in Connecticut. So now she's out of the city which is what she had wanted so much. But when I found myself sharing a mirror with her in the ladies' room after a fund-raiser for the public library, I saw that her charisma had vanished. Her beautiful, arrogant face had aged prematurely into something rigid and cynical, and the magnificent hair was dry and cut in a skimpy, mannish style. It wouldn't be fair to attribute Isabel's transformation to Joy, but it's tempting.

And finally, one afternoon when I was picking Roberta up from school, Mary Farrar approached me and suggested we have lunch. It seemed Joy had dumped her the week before for a young popular male agent from California.

Poor Mary had gone the limit to get Joy the biggest possible advance for her third, very awful, book, *A Kid from Jersey*. In addition to providing Joy with room and board for months, Mary had bought her clothes, entertained her friends and, I believe, even slept with her. (Unlike Ralph, Mary's husband had been immune to Joy's seductions and had threatened divorce several times during her sojourn in their apartment.)

I managed not to say I told you so and nodded sympathetically. But Mary wasn't seeking sympathy. After listing all the services she had rendered to Joy and all the insults she'd received in return, the only thing she wanted to know from me was: What did I think she had done to offend Joy and was there any way she could make it up to her?

I never felt qualified to give Joy's victims an opinion and didn't. I'd just listen as closely as I used to listen to Joy so many years before. There was something to be learned from all this other than cynicism. I was sure of it.

After the publication of *A Kid from Jersey,* which was a critical and commercial failure, Joy disappeared. Some said she was in Europe, others believed she had set up house with a Chinese businessman in Hong Kong. But I learned from Mary Farrar, who never stopped inquiring after her, that she was actually in India.

It was also Mary who told me, somewhere around 1981, that a new manuscript of Joy's, about the rich and decadent in New Delhi, was being circulated among publishers by a little-known agent who represented English-speaking Asiatic authors.

The book eventually came out as an original paperback in 1983. I borrowed a copy from Mary. It was even worse than the third book. None of it made sense. The story was buried in so many verbless sentences and parenthetical statements about the narrator's personal misery that you couldn't make out what the characters were doing, much less what sex they were, since all had four-syllable Indian names except for the li'l' Joy character, whose name was Baby Fauntleroy.

People said she was taking drugs. Uppers and downers and hashish. Nothing in the book gave me reason to disbelieve that.

After I'd read, or tried to read, that fourth book, I pretty well forgot about Joy. No one heard from her or talked about her. When I ran into the talk show host one afternoon on Fifth Avenue, he said that Joy had obviously gone to join her friends, the lost and the mad.

And my life went on. I lived as a divorcée, alone with the children, and didn't hate it nearly as much as I thought I would, but then, I was still in my thirties, decently provided for—though I did have to supplement my income with free-lance advertising—and had dieted down to a size ten.

This would be around the same time Marisa started making her two-month trips to Cameroon to study the Baka in the rain forest. Joy tells me she learned their language. I can picture Marisa—khaki shorts, simple polo shirt, dark-blond hair tied in a ponytail—visiting their tribal villages. She is sitting on a camp stool, her tape recorder on a fold-out table, going over the elementary vocabulary of the tiny, gentle tribespeople around her. Taking notes, thinking hard, she is trying to discover in this simple, rude society how and why her own culture has moved from such original simplicity and orderliness to what it is now.

I wonder, Does Marisa see our culture as I do? Does she see the cruelty and feel the absence of gods—the female ones—as I do?

Is this why I paint insects? I wish I could stop painting them, but they keep insisting, buzzing and batting themselves against the walls of my imagination. I've just finished a series of hornets which will never sell to anyone. Who would hang them in their home? Perhaps the hornets are my metaphor for the violence I see everywhere, on television, in the news-papers, in the way people speak. But I am digressing.

In 1984, I married Kenneth Royden, a widower without

children who is a brilliant architect and ten years older than me. He is good-natured, solidly talented and the man I should have married in the first place. He is also fun to be with and possessed of a definite weakness for and appreciation of women, especially their more unpredictable aspects.

My parents were thrilled when they met him and made no effort to disguise their gratitude to him for "saving" their daughter. From what? Myself, I guess.

Somewhere around the time of my marriage I began selling my paintings—of the flowers and fruits, not the insects—to a small, discerning (in my opinion) group of friends and collectors who put them on the walls of their hallways and bedrooms. A health-food restaurant in SoHo and a country furniture store on the East Side have also bought a few.

I am not a success in either the commercial or critical sense. Perhaps because for so long I never dared to hope I would be. My only real success—thus far—consists in finding out what I like to do most and then doing it.

These first four years of marriage have been the happiest, most fulfilling in my life. My children admire and obey me and are doing well in school. My husband thinks I am talented and sexy and a catch. And we have more friends and money between us than we ever dreamed of having.

I think it's because I've been feeling so blissful, so confident, that when Joy, home at last from India, called me a month ago, I didn't cut her off, but hung on and listened as she begged my forgiveness for what had happened so many years before with Ralph. She was out of her mind in those days, she said, and already on drugs—really, really miserable.

But all that was behind her now. She was clean, wanted to mend bridges and start down a new path. She had thought of me so many times. She had always liked me more than any of her other friends. She had seen my paintings in the SoHo restaurant and was amazed at my progress. I was a real artist now. Did I know that? God, living outside the U.S.

was a mistake. She had missed it so much, would never leave New York again and adored the little apartment on 107th Street and Broadway she had rented. She had finally grown up, but felt younger than she ever had felt before. Did I know what she meant? Damn, but she would give anything to see someone intelligent and talented and, you know, sensitive, like myself. Would I meet her just once, anywhere I liked, anytime?

After about fifteen minutes of that, I heard myself inviting her to have lunch with me at the Sign of the Dove.

FIVE

She was already seated in the dining room and talking earnestly to the busboy when I arrived at the restaurant. Spiffily dressed in a mauve YSL coat, skirt and lavishly bowed silk blouse, she looked much the same. Definitely younger than forty-two. The roundness of her face helps, as do the small, retroussé nose, feathery blond hair—which hasn't a strand of gray—and the smooth, youthful hands with their exquisitely buffed nails. (She still eschews nail polish.) Even her smile has retained most of its infantile appeal. Though, I must say, it didn't seem to be turning on the busboy, who looked more than a little relieved to get away once he had pulled out my chair.

We ordered champagne cocktails—her new drink, she said—and for the first half hour, she preyed upon my compassion nonstop, beginning with a nostalgic account of the old days when she could afford to take whole parties of people to the Sign of the Dove. In that golden era, she had apparently been more generous with her time and money than Mother Teresa and the heirs of John D. Rockefeller combined.

From there, she went on to describe her horrendous second marriage to Frederick Worth, who had betrayed her and taken all her significant money. The lawyer who represented her had not, it appeared, been as astute as Ralph. I didn't ask if he was anybody's husband. I didn't ask anything that might lead to a confrontation. I just listened, suspended belief and bided my time. For what? I didn't know.

The rest of her money had evaporated in India. Though she had gone there for spiritual inspiration, she had not mixed with the ragged remnants of the hippie drug culture still extant in Goa and Nepal. No indeed. She had known maharanis. One of whom was an eminent lesbian, who introduced her to Just Everyone in New Delhi. There followed capsule descriptions of the palaces she had stayed in and a titillating story about the Gandhi family which I don't dare repeat.

After the maharani, she had a long affair with an Indian Moslem and might even have married him, but you never knew about the four-wives thing; much as she loved women, she just couldn't . . . but his home, my God, Madeleine, gold goblets for everyday wine, bathrooms the size of living rooms, servants constantly bowing and scraping and begging to do everything but brush her teeth for her. And the *jewels*. She'd learned *all* about precious gems—what was good, what wasn't—and would teach me if I liked.

I was, as usual, mesmerized, but tried valiantly not to show it. Partly because, as a serious artist, I felt I should now be above this kind of patter, but mostly because I was afraid of getting sucked in again.

After we had ordered lunch, I asked instead about her present situation. It's great, just great, she said, and her face sagged with sadness. I ignored the sadness and pressed for more information.

Well, she adored living on West 107th Street. People were so real there, she said, disposing of the sorrowful look and firming her chin in a courage-under-stress mode.

She had started mixing with all kinds of women writers,

famous writers, she said, and rolled their names off her tongue as though describing the ingredients of some rare Romanian stew, but her heart wasn't in it. In truth, she confessed, these women had forced her to rethink her own writing and slightly, maybe a little bit, downwardly mobile career. Maybe her talent was gone, she said stoically. Maybe she really should stop writing altogether. Since I more or less agreed, I of course remained silent.

The notable omission in all this was sex. In the old days, her narrations had always been peppered with this and that perversion. A ten-minute segment didn't go by without someone, usually her, getting beaten up or gang banged in two or more orifices. But in this age of AIDS, promiscuity is as out of date as ponchos. Never one to buck a powerful trend, Joy has learned to soft-pedal her appalling appetite for anal sex or any other activities that might draw blood.

The way she had it in her mind that afternoon, she had been as puritanical a product of Middle-American morality as I had been. The snorting, tearing orgies of the past, which I couldn't help reminding her of, had become fictionalized, which is to say, they were only in her books and had never happened. Hadn't I realized that? she asked, lifting the little vase of anemones in the center of the table and tickling her nose with them. "I never really, *really* tell the truth."

And who knows? Maybe she doesn't. But I wouldn't bet on it.

Toward dessert—Tarte Tatin slathered with Crème Anglaise—she told me about the new man she had met in her building, Scott Arnold, formerly of western Connecticut. Had I ever run into him? No? Well, he knew a lot of important builders and real-estate men whom Kenneth might want to meet.

That was when she gave me all the facts about their first meeting, which I described at the start of this story—or whatever you want to call this piece of writing which I am taking precious painting time to put down on paper. I'm still not sure why I'm doing this.

Because I think there's more to learn from her? Or because, by recording all the facts, I hope I'll hit upon a way to take revenge against her for destroying my first marriage? But I'm glad now to be divorced from Ralph and married to Kenneth. Then what is it I want from her? Maybe just to listen to her.

She is truly a wonderful storyteller. In another age, she would have been a troubadour. I can picture her, going from court to court, enchanting the assembled lords and ladies with tales of buggery, rape and greed, strumming her lyre with an anguished smile.

"Tell me more about Marisa," I said. "I'm fascinated by her. What did she do to him that was so awful?"

"From what I can make out, the worst thing she did was not do what he wanted."

"Like what?"

"Like not make him breakfast."

"That's all?"

"He also didn't like her taking those trips to Cameroon to study the Pygmies. And then, when she refused to get rid of the servants—"

"Why get rid of the servants?"

"Because he wanted her to be a regular wife. To take care of him."

"You mean wash out his socks?"

"And the toilets." She laughed. "That's what they want, you know. Why do you think servants have been gradually disappearing since the beginning of the century?"

"Because of welfare. Poor people saw they could get money for not working, so naturally they decided not to work in other people's houses."

She laughed. "True, but isn't it odd that just as women

started getting educated and really threatening men, welfare just happened to come along?"

"That doesn't mean men *wanted* servants to disappear."

"All I know is that a woman pushing a vacuum cleaner around is a lot less of a threat than one telling her gardener and cook what to do and then going upstairs to her study to write her Ph.D. thesis on Pygmies."

I was amazed. In all the years I'd known Joy, she'd never come up with anything this close to being a genuine feminist thought. "Where did you get all this?"

"By looking around and seeing what's going on. In the old days, middle-class women in America had whole household staffs, but the minute they started getting a little power and bringing home real money and getting uppity, they suddenly had to do all their own housework."

"What about those yuppie women whose husbands cook and do the laundry?"

"Have you ever seen one do his share except on TV shows, which always turn out to be written by a woman?"

"You really think men *like* to see their wives scrubbing floors?"

"Maybe not. They may even feel guilty. But unconsciously all men want their wives to be so busy waiting on them—so demeaned—they never develop into a threat. Which is why most women writers and painters who are married are generally such mediocre artists."

Pow. The ultimate counter-flat. I really don't know why I'm bothering with her.

SIX

Ever since our lunch at the Sign of the Dove, it's been like old times. Joy is out in the world hunting for prey and coming back to report to me at the cave, where I've been tending to the arts, my man and my children. She gives me a progress report on her affair with Scott almost every other day.

Unfortunately, it all comes through in her new bowdlerized narrative style. Although they are enjoying sexual intercourse practically every night, she describes this event in banal terms. Everything is delicious, divine, tender etc. Though she is still heavily into pitifulness, her taste for perversity has definitely dried up. Now all she talks about are conversational nuances, small gestures and strategic moves.

A couple of weeks ago Scott indicated that he wanted her to cook dinner for him. Question: Should she create a Mexican dinner featuring raw green chiles that will have him gagging and gargling mouthwash for a week and will therefore discourage all further requests for home cooking or should she whip up Julia Childs's recipe for delicious Suprèmes de Volaille with rare imported mushrooms in a Madeira-drenched cream sauce?

"The chicken. Do the chicken," I say from my camp fire.

I am being sincere. I cook dinner for Kenneth three or four nights a week, not because he has a cliché notion that food equals love, but because he is a 1980s man and wants a wife who gives good value. In other words, home-cooked meals equal service which he has paid for, since his work brings in money and mine brings in practically none. Make of that what you will.

I also want to think of her over there on 107th Street in her kitchen, scattered and sweating, with pots boiling over and pans burning. I want her to be so distraught and hot she forgets to pitch her voice an octave higher than any grown woman I've ever known.

In the end, she decides to do the Mexican meal. Results are as predicted. He takes three mouthfuls, stops breathing, drinks a quart of water and gobbles up a whole loaf of French bread she has coated in garlic butter. The next morning, he howls like a wolf when his bowel movement sears his sphincter muscles so badly that his long-dormant hemorrhoids start bleeding. She mentions this now-taboo region of the body in a naughty whisper, followed by a naughtier giggle.

He never asks her to cook again and has fallen into the habit of taking her to a nice little restaurant in the neighborhood which caters to unmarried yuppies who have been forced into the region by the high rents on the Upper East Side. With her encouragement, he has managed to put on ten pounds: "And, oh Madeleine, he looks so cute with his little tummy. I adore men with a little weight on them."

She would prefer to effect this fattening-up process at "21," but, she says, it's still a hell of a lot better than standing in front of her refrigerator eating ice cream, which is what she was doing most nights before she met him.

"If you don't cook for him, he may leave you the way he left Marisa," I warn her the next time she calls. I am standing in the kitchen, the phone tucked between my chin and my shoulder, washing and wiping my long-stemmed crystal wine-glasses, which the cleaning woman refuses to touch. "At least, if your theory that men want a woman serving them is right."

"My theory is right and I *am* serving him. I'm going to be his mentor."

It seems that lately he has been putting pressure on her to keep her promise to show one of her friends in publishing his awful book. If she doesn't do it, she could very well lose him. "I'm thinking of giving it to Franny Fagen at Towne Publishing."

"Can you trust her?" I ask.

"Implicitly. She's my oldest, dearest friend in publishing."

Which could mean she met her at a party last week or they had an affair of several months.

"Well, if you trust her, tell her to keep the manuscript for three weeks and during that time, push Scott like crazy to get a job," I advise her. For reasons that still elude me, I am dedicated to helping her ensnare this Scott Arnold and some-how turn him into a wage earner again. Maybe because I like her more these days. Or maybe I'm afraid that if she doesn't land Scott, she'll ask me for money and I'll end up giving it to her.

She's having a bit of a cash flow problem, she says. In fact, she can't even pay next month's rent. She was banking on picking up some money from a lecture tour in New England, but her lecture agent had to cancel her tour because the market for grotesque sex has apparently dried up.

"Tell him the only way to get his mind off the book is to make phone calls and go out on interviews," I kibitz from my kitchen. "If he ends up getting a job, the book may take a backseat in his mind. But if he doesn't get a job, tell this Franny Fagen to return the manuscript saying she finds it riveting, but wants him to rewrite the whole thing."

"Why?"

"The thought of rewriting two thousand pages will be so horrendous he will try even harder to get a job."

"Yeah, but then he will probably want me to rewrite it."

"So why don't you?"

"Because it is the most awful piece of crap I've ever read. I know you don't think much of me as a writer, but I do know good from bad and this is horrible."

"Then say you can't rewrite it because you're too busy with your own book."

"Oh God, that's another problem. He keeps asking to read my new book, but I've only written fifty pages of it. Which, of course, I haven't told him."

"How is it?"

"Dirty."

Which, coming from her, can only mean truly revolting.

"Why don't you quickly write something else?" I ask.

"I can't. I've told you a million times, I'm blocked."

"Get unblocked," I reply unhelpfully. "Write a Gothic novel. Pretend you are Daphne du Maurier."

"Mmm. Yes." Long pause as she considers this suggestion seriously. "That's not a bad idea. If I tried to do a sort of parody, I might be able to pull it off. One thing I haven't lost is my gift for plotting."

Suddenly I'm afraid she really can do such a novel and will get rich again, famous, free and happy again. But no, not possible. She is far too obsessed with her own druggy, devious self to devote a whole book to a woman who is as naive, virtuous and faithful as a Gothic heroine.

"Well, do it really fast," I say. "He may get suspicious if you delay too long."

"I don't know if I can. I'm such a slow typist."

"I know a diet doctor who still gives Dexedrine to special patients."

"No. I've given all that up."

I know this can't be true. When she calls, she is entirely too good-humored. No woman her age, living on the brink of destitution and possibly jail, could stay in such a good mood without popping a few controlled substances.

Or maybe she is not on the brink of destitution, as she claims. She is perfectly capable of mattressing some cash in a Swiss bank account that one of her maharanis has opened for her which she has failed to mention.

Who knows about anything with her?

"Well, try the Gothic book. It might be fun," I say, but the thought of her struggling to create long, flowery descriptions of nineteenth-century stately homes and respectful servants as she sits in her three-and-a-half-room pad makes me wince.

In the end, she follows my advice somewhat. She gives Scott's two thousand pages to Franny, but tells her nothing about her plot to hook Scott.

"I don't have to explain anything to her," she says to me when I next see her.

She is standing with her back to me, looking out the window of my apartment on East Seventy-fifth Street. Have I mentioned that when I married Kenneth, I moved uptown to a place twice the size of my old one? That it is a duplex with a huge fourth bedroom upstairs which I use as my studio? And that the size of my canvases has increased from two-by-twos to three-by-sixes and that we are thinking of buying some land in the Hamptons and building a summer house?

This is the first time I have invited her home since our lunch at the Sign of the Dove five months ago. Which is not very nice of me inasmuch as she has already had me up to her place on 107th Street—bare floors, director's chairs, card tables and a round bed that's seven feet in diameter—but she makes no mention of my lack of hospitality. She just compliments me profusely on our stylish gray-on-gray-on-charcoal living room which Kenneth designed and decorated himself, right down to the gleaming porcelain ashtrays. All of which makes the room impossible to relax in. But since it's not for relaxing, but for showcasing Kenneth's talent, I have managed to adjust—and restore the balance by maintaining our bedroom and my studio in a state of sumptuous disorder.

"When Franny Fagen reads Scott's book," she says, raising one of the pale-gray roman shades which cover our bay windows, "she'll know it's about a man who just left his wife and she'll understand right away why I'm trying to get his novel sold."

I draw in my breath, startled by her subtlety in dealing with this Franny. I am so used to thinking of Joy as superficial and self-involved that I have forgotten she is an expert in dealing with the unexplained and unspoken in her relationships with others. What does she know but has not mentioned about my state of mind?

"Oh look, there's a nanny down there pushing such an adorable baby in a carriage," she says, pointing down at the street. I join her at the window. The early spring sun is making the pavement sparkle and the trees that line the street are covered with fresh green buds. A beautiful chubby baby looks up and gurgles happily at the sky, perhaps at us. I glance at Joy. Her face is collapsing with longing as she gazes down at the child.

She turns and faces me with mournful eyes. "I wish I had a child of my own. Oh, how I wish."

"Maybe you still can."

"No."

"Do you still have regular periods?"

"Yes."

"Why don't you try having a baby with Scott? There are lots of women your age who are having babies these days. They've got all sorts of new ways of monitoring fertility and—"

"And what if it turned out to have Down's syndrome?"

Her use of the proper term for what most people our age still lazily call "mongolism" is not like her. I wonder if she has already looked into this question of having a baby.

"They have that test," I say. "Amniocentesis. It can tell whether the baby is normal when you're in your fourth or fifth month."

"I know. And if it isn't normal, the doctor kills it while it's still in your womb. He won't give you a cesarean and kill it himself because he's too moral for that. So you have to give birth to it dead. And they won't knock you out because they need you to be awake for contractions. It's the most agonizing thing a woman can go through. It happened to a friend of mine."

Which meant it had happened to her? Out there, somewhere in New Mexico or India? It's possible. I don't want to know.

I don't want to start pitying her again and anyhow, she hasn't asked for pity. She says it happened to a friend. Also, for a woman in her early forties to try to ensnare a fifty-year-old man with pregnancy is lunacy and the worst of all my unhelpful suggestions.

My desire to wish her ill falters. At least I no longer want to avenge myself for having been taken advantage of so often. I may even be starting to forgive her.

Certainly I feel for her almost as much as I would for my daughter, Roberta, if she were to be subjected to such a grotesque ordeal or unable to have a baby when she wanted to. Though I'm inclined to think Joy really could have had children; that the pill and the various abortions she herself chose to have, and not the back-street abortion her mother supposedly forced upon her when she was sixteen, are the real reasons she didn't. I have a feeling she made a conscious choice, long before she met Geoffrey Castleman, to live by her wits and not get involved with the toil and responsibility of child raising. And now, because she regrets this decision,

I pity her. At heart, I think she is like any other woman and genuinely wishes she had a couple of kids to love and mold in her image.

I can just see them: two little teenage girls—they would have to be girls—with high-pitched voices and round cunning faces, manipulating their peers into giving them what they don't deserve, haven't earned. How they would love Joy, laugh with her, scheme. One would already be writing a short-story collection. The other would carry condoms in her Filofax when she went to parties and would know about entitlement and lawsuits and pass along insider information.

"Where are your kids now?" she asks.

I look at my watch. "Roberta is still in school. She'll be home at four if she doesn't stay late with the debating society."

"And Harold?"

"He's at Choate. I thought I told you."

"He got into Choate?"

I nod happily. "He's smart."

"When does Kenneth come home?"

"He went to Kansas City for a meeting about some museum they're building."

"Oh."

I look away. There's too much anguish in her fidgeting hands. She isn't crying, fighting tears or indulging in any of her usual antics. She is looking stonily at the Brancusi sculpture, Kenneth's most prized possession, gleaming from its marble pedestal.

Christ, I am privileged! How is it that fate decided that I be fruitful and blessed with so many of life's gifts and Joy be so deprived? Because she deserves it? Because she has no heart, the absence of which mysteriously kills fetuses before birth?

But that heartlessness could be a product of fate. Had I been raised by Maddy Bolingbroke and Terence Claire, perhaps I too would behave as she does/did. Maybe she really isn't to blame.

Who am I to figure out such matters? I only do fruits and flowers and bugs.

"I know both of them will turn out to be wonderful kids," she says to me. There is none of the cloying flattery I know so well sugaring her voice. This is an unadorned statement, devoid of emotion or an ulterior strategy. She has failed. I have won.

I, an artist of no repute, a child of the heartlands, fruit of a home deprived of stars and scandal, have grateful children, a husband who loves me and money in my bank account. Every morning, I wake up happy, make coffee in my overly designed kitchen and drink it while I read the *Times* in our monochrome living room, the coldness of which I successfully ignore.

While, at the same hour, far across town, this lonely, childless opportunist before me stirs her instant coffee in a cracked mug, hoping against hope that she can resuscitate her old skills and trap the man upstairs who may well be more of a mid-life failure than she is.

Though she has often described Scott with his Gregory Peck face and independent mind as "God, really sort of a natural aristocrat," I have already concluded that he is, more than anything, an opportunist.

Born in Mississippi, of lower-middle-class stock, he has done very well for himself since he left home. Getting the imperial Marisa to marry him must have demanded talents equal to, if not greater, than Joy's. That this northern heiress threw this Snopes character (traveling in reverse, as it were) out after their children were grown is not surprising. (I have long ago decided that his story that their breakup was "mutual" is a lie. What man writes two thousand pages about a woman he has walked out on?) What is surprising is that he lasted in her house of many lawns and servants for twenty-six years. It may well be that Joy has met her match at last.

Though these are all just guesses on my part, since I have not yet met him. I very much want to. Possibly he would make some unguarded statement that would validate these assumptions of mine. But Joy has not offered to introduce me to him without Kenneth being there. And this, thus far, I have refused to do.

One of our unspoken understandings is that I do not trust her to be in the same room with a husband of mine. (That she might accidentally run into Kenneth was my main reason for waiting so long before inviting her to our apartment.) Her repeated suggestions that we four meet at "some nice place one night" and all her fluttery hints that Scott Arnold knows important businessmen searching for an architect to build multimillion dollar shopping malls have fallen on deaf ears.

I realize that preventing her from meeting Kenneth is a kind of punishment. By withholding trust, the very material with which she erects her elaborate cons, I am hurting her— at the very least, annoying her. In a way, I feel guilty about this, like a rich woman keeping back food from the starving. But not guilty enough. Let her starve. Or let her go and feed on some other woman's trust. If she can. I have a feeling she can't.

I have a feeling that the trees have grown sparser in her Sherwood Forest. There are fewer hiding places and fewer travelers in the late eighties. The culture she preyed upon so skillfully has caught up with her at last. She is no longer ahead of the times, but of them. She is stuck in the middle of an era as heartless as she. And is eight pounds overweight with nothing to offer but her fading fame and frivolous dreams.

And I, who need nothing, am at the pinnacle of the female heap. My suffering is long gone. I have found contentment.

Have I become heartless too?

Perhaps and be that as it may. My ambivalence is inexcusable, but I am not looking for excuses. I am writing all this down so I can figure out what is going on here. In my heart. In our lives.

"I don't understand why Scott doesn't get hired by someone," she says, turning away from the window and sitting on the charcoal couch. All her analytical powers are focused on this problem and her smooth white hands have stopped fidgeting.

"He spent this whole week calling people and meeting them. I did as you suggested, by the way, and told him to really throw himself into job hunting while he waits to hear from Franny about his book. But I'm wondering if all his phone calls and stuff are doing any good."

"I bet it's the first time he has really tried to get work."

"No, he's been trying for months and months. He showed me some of the letters he's written to companies and headhunters."

"Are you sure you know the real reason why he was fired?"

"He wasn't fired, just let go when his company was taken over. It's true. I saw the newspaper articles describing the takeover fight."

"Is it possible that he isn't really trying to get a job? That he secretly wants to live off the interest on his savings and write full time?"

"I hope not. For his sake, not just for mine." She crosses her legs and purses her lips in a worried adult fashion. "I've been wondering if there is something wrong with him that I don't see."

"What do you mean?"

"Oh, some tic or mannerism that puts businessmen off. Something which I, being a writer, just can't recognize. What if he sounds unreliable or something? To me, he comes across like Iacocca compared to my husbands or my, you know, women. But what do I know?"

And then I'm saying "I bet Kenneth could tell if he does anything wrong."

"Really? I wonder. Architects are artists more than businessmen, aren't they?"

"True, but Kenneth has to deal with businessmen all day. He knows good ones from bad ones." Which is why he is so successful.

"Do you think if he saw Scott he could judge how he came across in business interviews?"

"Maybe."

This is my cue to suggest that we all get together. I have fallen into her trap. It is only fitting that I close the door after me. But I am determined not to make it that easy for her. "I'll talk to him about it and see if he's willing to put himself on the line and actually *judge* Scott."

"I'd be so grateful." She knows I am faking and will deliver up Kenneth within a week. She looks distractedly for her purse. Now that her mission—to break me down to the point where I offer to introduce Scott to Kenneth—has been achieved, she has suddenly decided to go home. For if she stays, there's a chance Roberta will burst in upon us, her cheeks rosy from the walk home from school, long, silky hair shining between little hair combs, happy, preppy voice and wondrous grace sending shock waves through the charcoal and gray living room.

And Joy will find herself obliged to flatter and coo and carry on about how wonderful my daughter is, how happy she is for me, all the while feeling the most wrenching envy she has ever felt in her life.

Which is why she is clutching her purse. For inside it I know there is a pill that, once she is out the door and waiting for the elevator in the hall, she will slip into her mouth to ease the pain this projected envy has caused.

I have no regrets, repeat, no regrets, for having given in to her regarding the Kenneth-Scott meeting. As I stated above, I've been wanting to meet Scott myself for some time and the simplest way to achieve this is to bring Kenneth into the picture. And actually, what have I to lose? Kenneth? To this sad, wandering-eyed woman baby?

Please.

"What are you going to do after Franny rejects Scott's book?" I ask as she rises from the sofa. "Are you going to offer to rewrite it or are you going to start the Gothic novel?"

"Neither." She grins mischievously and starts walking toward the door. "I have a better plan."

"Oh?"

"In exactly two weeks, I'm calling Franny and asking her to tell Scott that he's wildly talented and his book is terrific."

"And then?"

"But—and here's the catch—to tell him that the book is *so* good it doesn't have broad appeal and she can't get Towne to back it. Which means that even if it gets published, it will sink without a trace. He'll be so mortified by the idea of writing a book no one ever hears about I'm sure he'll decide to hell with it and withdraw it."

"What if he doesn't? What if he says 'Thank you very much, I'd like you to publish it even if only a few people read it'?"

"He won't. After almost six months of sleeping with him, Madeleine, I know something about the man. I know ego when I see it."

"What if he decides to forget about looking for a job and tries to write a new book, a real potboiler, which Towne would back?"

"He will." Her pale eyes gleam with some of the old fire. "Many, many years from now. After he has retired. With my help."

And I had thought she had met her match in Scott.

SEVEN

I made a reservation for dinner on Tuesday for the four of us at the Metropolitan Club. Why not, I thought, give one of her Yves Saint Laurent ensembles an outing in the robber-baron air of that overdone place? It's fun to gawk at the gilt and grandeur, the rococo ceilings and portraits of the eminent founders: Morgan, West et al. There's a lot those stern, well-fed patriarchs could teach Joy and her paramour. Namely, how, once you've got it, it's okay to flaunt it, but hold on to some of it too for God's sake. Don't you know the hounds move in on your sort when you're down and they're up?

I am a little drunk and very tired. We just got home and I am in my studio writing because I can't sleep. I am also afraid.

What's new about that? I've always been afraid of many things: rape, muggers in Central Park, random killers, the bomb, the poorhouse, but tonight I am afraid of myself.

Last night I had a nightmare: I am in the backyard of our house on Elm Street that I grew up in. It is night and there is no moon. It is as black and dark as Kenneth's and my bedroom when the blinds and double-lined curtains are drawn. I can see only the dimmest outline of our old large, wood-framed house and can barely make out the backstairs leading to the kitchen. The grass is as black as the dirt. The gravel in the driveway looks like coal chips. "There is nothing here," I say to myself, "just darkness." Then behind me, terrifyingly, a car approaches. Its headlights are illuminating my face, the house, the yard. I smile bravely and, pretending to be busy opening a door, I try to ignore the blinding white beams.

What darkness in my mind has yet to come to light? I asked myself as I woke up sweating, thirsty and cold.

I lay there for a while, listening to Kenneth's steady breathing, and tried to get back enough composure to spend the rest of the night in bed.

But when I closed my eyes, a beautiful woman in a white, pure silk dress—French-cut sleeves, loose folds, gold buttons—drifted into my imagination.

She is sitting at a small, leather-topped secretary with curved Queen Anne legs. A lock of dark-blond hair falls across her forehead. She fiddles with the pen in her hand. Then, finding her thought, she writes it down quickly. She is doing an assignment for her Master's in anthropology.

Through the window, there are sounds of children laughing and playing and the smart crack of a croquet ball being hit by a mallet. She looks down and smiles. Her two beautiful sons are playing croquet on the lawn under the watchful eye of their nanny.

She looks at her watch. Twelve-thirty. Time to stop working and have lunch. She presses a button on the wall near the desk—her signal to the cook that she is ready for lunch.

Leaving her sun-filled office, she passes through a corridor filled with sculptures on heavy columns. At the head of the wide, circular stairs is a half-round table with a giant urn of long-stemmed spring flowers. She walks down the stairs, through the marble-floored reception hall and into the dining room, which looks out onto a wide green lawn and ancient trees. The children are summoned and they join her at the table with the nanny.

They have soup, then vegetables with some light broiled fish and a compote of fruit for dessert, served by the genial, much-loved butler who has worked for her family since she was a child. It is he who drives her into Manhattan every other day, where she attends classes at Columbia while the children are in school.

She asks for coffee to be brought to her office. No, she has coffee at the table, then takes a walk around the grounds while the children take their nap. She is no longer in a white dress now, but dressed in riding clothes—a simple Irish knit sweater, jodhpurs and dark-brown boots.

Yes, she rides every other day. She takes out her horse, a beautiful chestnut mare, and canters through the western Connecticut countryside with its gray stone walls and rolling hills.

Oh, dear Marisa, who inspires no guilt and asks for no pity. So far from all of us. From Joy, scrounging around for a man to save her. From successful, childless Isabel Swann, whose beauty is gone. From the exhausted Mary Farrar, who is almost an old woman now.

Can Marisa be real? Must she be as far away as those long-ago goddesses . . . Diana, Astarte, Isis or the really glorious, ancient ones like Nammu and my favorite of all, Eurynome, "whose dance separated light from darkness, sea from sky."

God, there were so many of them. Real heroines. Women worth worshiping. Why have they all gone away? Why don't people, or at least women, remember them?

How can I make Marisa real?

Kenneth moved onto his back. His breathing turned to snores.

Marisa is cantering lightly down a narrow bridle path, past

thick-trunked trees with young spring leaves. Her clean, dark-blond hair flies carelessly in the wind and caresses her slender neck as she takes a jump over a low stone wall.

After her bath and a few more hours of work at her desk, she will have dinner by candlelight with Scott and talk a little too much about the rain forests, the tiny Baka and the ways of innocent people while Scott sits sullenly, silently, waiting for her to shut up, wishing she were leaning over a stove, face flushed from the heat of greasy food fumes, serving him his dinner, jumping up and down, bringing in more food, running back to the kitchen for the butter which I always forget. Or the pepper mill. In fact, standing through much of the meal. Having earlier walked down West Eleventh street, back bent, knees tired, pulling a grocery cart, the kids straggling behind me, tearing at the cookies I just bought at the supermarket, then darting ahead and nearly giving me a heart attack because I think they won't stop at the light.

I hoped to be an artist and do all that! Oh, maybe I could have, if I were a genius or, like Joy and Isabel, not had children. Or abandoned them.

But God, no. I wanted Roberta and Harold. I love them.

Kenneth's snores turned to snorts: a loud, staccato *gchwahh*. The silence between them varied from twenty to fifty seconds. During the silences I sent up little pleas to the demons who were causing them. But they wouldn't stop tormenting him. I moved him onto his side. Silence for about a minute. And then he or the demons were at it again. It was driving me mad.

I wanted to wake him up, pound his back, bellow and stomp around the bedroom like a madwoman. Like a madwoman who had been in the attic too long. But what I did was go down the hall to Harold's empty room, throw back the tweedy bedspread of his single bed and fling myself into it.

Curled in a ball, I tried to calm myself, think happy

thoughts. In the morning, the cleaning woman was coming.

I am no longer a full-time servant, thank you, but a part-time one. And no, I'm not really in the market for a butler today.

Where was I?

At the Metropolitan Club. Yes. Tonight, we took Joy and Scott to the Metropolitan Club. Joy looked smashing in a black velvet dress. Scott was handsome in a gray pinstriped suit that would have looked better if it had been a size larger.

Joy liked Kenneth, paid him the great compliment of listening to him when he spoke and not looking around at the other diners. She also did not flirt with him. Her treatment of him was not dissimilar to the way I treat Ralph Tyson these days: with an intelligent, straightforward awareness that it pays to stay on the good side of the father of my children.

On the other hand, she was all cuddles and sweetness with Scott. Nothing in her manner suggested she was capable of the hard-boiled analysis she'd made of him and his marriage a few days before. "Isn't he as handsome as I said he was?" she whispered loudly to me when we met in the cavernous downstairs bar. Then: "Don't you love his smile?" It was his last smile.

Upstairs in the dining room: "Scott, tell them about the time you went over your boss's head and made five million dollars for DPL in 1982." Before we ordered our food: "Scott, do your imitation of George Bush defending his honor on TV."

Scott manfully ignored these coy requests but did not succeed in resisting the forkfuls of curried chicken she had ordered for herself which she periodically shoved into his mouth. Whether out of politeness or real hunger, he managed to eat his entire beef Wellington and four fifths of her meal, all the while trying to carry on some semblance of adult conversation with Kenneth. Mostly they discussed the economy and politics. Scott held his own and did not appear to be as much of a philistine as I'd anticipated.

He pretty much ignored me, the crucial intermediary for this meal, but Joy had warned me that he tended to view most women as superfluous. Though when we were ordering dessert, he did pay attention when I rather nastily suggested that, since the club's portions of Sacher torte were small, he should order cheesecake instead.

Kenneth's opinion after we put them in a cab: "He sure was hungry." When I pressed for a more detailed analysis: "He seems like a good guy. Nothing I can see that's wrong with him, but the job market's tight for a man his age."

My darling, brilliant Kenneth, who can make steel soar with the grace of a swan and create shopping malls people call visionary, is no talker.

He is direct, honest, generous and a little balding. He is the husband all my divorced friends dream of marrying, and I am incredibly lucky to have found him, but he is also loath to gossip or criticize people and he never, *never* sticks his neck—broad, spilling ever so slightly over his collar—out when it comes to those whom he considers to be in my sphere of influence.

And Joy, he has decided, is definitely in my sphere. She is my problem, my nutsiness. (I have told him about Ralph's night with her and Isabel.) After meeting her and Scott, he has decided that he has no desire to get involved in their spiraling needs. He hasn't said this in so many words, but it's obvious that's how he feels.

His only explicit comment about Joy herself was "Maybe she was better looking when she was young." He also cannot fathom how Ralph, or any man, especially a man married to me, would want to share a vibrator with her.

I love Kenneth for these remarks and have not troubled to explain that Joy's success with my former husband and other men and women has never been based on her appearance, but on her ability to manipulate them.

But Kenneth, who is talented and attractive enough never to have to manipulate anyone—he gets just about anything he wants through plain asking—would never comprehend the value and scope of Joy's talents and I decide not to enlighten him. Instead, I tear into Scott, who is really a stiff. Far more inexpressive than I had expected.

Joy had already told me he tended to hide his emotions, but she had not prepared me for the actual degree of woodenness. Nor had she mentioned his fear. For that rigid supervision of his facial muscles can be caused only by fear. I smelled it the minute he walked into the dining room. Not fear of which fork to use or anything along those lines. Marisa had thoroughly educated him in this respect. And anyhow, all southerners are better mannered than northerners. No, this fear was coming from a deeper place.

Now, what does this have to do with my dream?

Nothing, I hope.

I am going to bed.

Today, Wednesday, Joy called to thank me for the *super* evening and to say that she thought Kenneth was "perfect for me." For a practiced flatterer, her choice of words to describe Kenneth showed remarkable restraint, but I understood her dilemma. If she went overboard about how fabulous he was, I might get suspicious and start thinking she was after him.

I liked this restraint and maintained it when I told her I thought Scott was "a very nice man" and that "Kenneth doesn't see anything wrong with him as far as his presentation of himself goes."

The phone went silent for about ten seconds. This was followed by an attack of coughing which sounded like the onset of tuberculosis.

"Are you all right?" I asked when the coughing subsided.

"Y-y-yes. I'm sorry. I was eating peanuts while I was talking to you and a bit of skin got caught in my throat. I didn't have any bread to make toast for breakfast. Well, anyhow, it was a great evening. I haven't been to the Metropolitan Club since I was a little girl."

"Well, the service is good."

"Did Kenneth say anything else about Scott or me?"

"No. Should he have? Oh yes, he thought you were great too."

"Really? That makes me feel better. I thought I'd made a bad impression."

She sounded so thrilled that I regretted having used the word "great." Which in fact Kenneth had not used. I had meant it to come out with a very small g, but she had blown it up to Great.

Joy, the Great Survivor.

"So, anyhow, let's keep in touch," I said in an attempt to close the conversation.

Another long pause on her end. I knew her mind was churning frantically. She didn't want to hang up before planting the thought that Kenneth should come up with a job lead for Scott. Because, you know, I am so lucky over here on Seventy-fifth Street with its elegant townhouses and nannies pushing baby carriages, while she is gazing down on panhandlers and junkies and inhaling bug spray fumes, not to mention eating peanuts for breakfast.

I let her churn. "How long before Franny Fagen returns Scott's book?" I asked.

"One week," she replied glumly.

"Well, it's possible he'll find a job before then."

"You don't find a job that quickly when you're at his level," she snapped.

She is slipping. Ten years ago, she never would have allowed herself to give the least sign of impatience or frustration when engaged in setting me, or any mark, up.

Could it be that Joy is becoming transparent?

If so, she'll end up a bag lady, before she is fifty. The image of her dragging a shopping cart through the streets with four coats on her back and chilblains on her legs, muttering celebrity names to herself, is not a wholly unwelcome one, but is too premature and guilt-provoking. No, far better to imagine her tidily ensconced with Scott in a little apartment in a three-story building in Queens, sitting on the stoop of a summer evening with all the neighborhood children gathered round, listening as she spins tales of a faraway time when little frogs like herself turned into semi-perverse princesses.

Or no, that isn't what I wish for.

I want her indebted, deeply indebted to me.

I want her giving *to me*.

And now I know at least one of the things I fear. I fear I am not nice. I fear that I am a grudge-keeper. I fear that I am losing my respect for myself.

If I belonged to a religion, I could go to church and pray away these thoughts. If I were in psychoanalysis, I could forget them in a great confessional outpouring. Or if I still did figure drawing, I could go upstairs and paint a portrait of Joy with snakes curling around her head. But I only paint fruits and flowers and insects. I haven't done figures since my first year in New York when I took life classes at the Art Students League.

So what does a person do when she thinks such terrible things about herself?

If she's me, she does more kind things, of course.

EIGHT

After that last phone call from Joy, I have heard nothing from her in several days. I feel vaguely disturbed by this. Has she given up on me as a conduit to her future happiness?

Today, while Kenneth was getting dressed to go to work, I asked him what he thought of her silence.

"She's embarrassed to call because Scott hasn't found a job yet," he replied.

"But Joy wants *you* to find Scott his job," I said.

Having slept badly the night before, I was still in bed, eating toast and drinking coffee.

He turned on his hair dryer and slicked back his hair, which is a soft brown color that compliments his warm, freckled skin. "She must have enough sense to know that an architect can't recommend a marketing man whom he barely knows for a job."

"You don't understand the way her mind works," I shouted over the sound of the dryer.

He turned off the dryer. "Who cares how her mind works?"

"She thinks you should help him because you should help *her* because she's about to go to jail."

"What do I care if she goes to jail?"

"Of all the things I've ever wished on her, I never wished she'd land in prison."

"Look, she's not my problem." He was getting upset. He didn't know how to respond to this meandering, hinting style of mine. He took a tie from the tie rack without bothering to look at the color and yanked it into a knot. The wide end fell below his belt.

"Here, let me help you," I said, getting out of bed and putting my arms around his neck.

He stepped away from me. "No, I can do it."

"Look. Don't be mad at *me*. I'm not asking you to help Scott. I know you can't," I said.

"Good."

"Anyhow, we can be sure we aren't the only people she's working over. She's probably talked a dozen friends into trying to get Scott a job. Though you are probably the most successful man she knows these days."

"She doesn't know me. I just met her."

"You're right. Forget I said anything." I kissed him on the cheek.

"You'll remember to call up the cleaners about my blue pinstripe for Friday?"

"Yes, darling." I caressed his arm.

"And you'll make a reservation for six on Friday at the Côte Basque and call back the real-estate agent in Bridgehampton about the two-acre lot on Mecox?"

"Yes, my love."

"Okay. Be sure to find out how far the land is from the ocean. I'll probably be home early. Around six."

"Are you still mad?"

"I'm not mad at all. I was never mad."

"Look, I don't care about Joy. I was just chatting, okay?"

"Okay." He put his arms around me, licked the side of my neck and kissed it.

A few minutes later, Roberta came in, borrowed my favorite black belt and also kissed me.

After they left, I tried to call Joy, but there was no answer. I got back into bed and tried to go back to sleep. But after forty, after breakfast you don't go back to sleep again. And Joy refused to get out of the forefront of my thoughts.

Supposing she is right. Supposing men want us middle-class women to be their servants to make sure they still control us and the world.

Which is why they brought welfare into being—unconsciously, of course. No one, not even the most rabid man hater, could claim it was intentional. But it *is* a coincidence that two of the most vital social changes in this century are equal rights for women and the gradual disappearance of servants.

And it is fairly amazing that a whole class of unskilled people, who might have been trained to become nannies and household servants, have had their incentive to work eroded by miserable little welfare stipends from a suddenly altruistic government.

The result: Women are allowed to be equal and "liberated"—they can even earn enormous salaries—as long as they are also tied down by housework, child raising and doing countless pride-stifling little tasks for their man. Thus leaving them without the time, energy or dignity to challenge male power in any substantive way.

Which is why you hear tired career women say (thoughtlessly, rather cruelly, I think) "I need a wife."

And in the end, nothing has really changed.

Men still have the real power, still run the world and, if I am to believe the statistics on the increase in rape and wife beating in America—and I do—are more violent than ever.

I fear men far more than I ever did when I was growing up in the late fifties and early sixties. Two decades of watching men in movies and on television rape and hit women, and shoot, bash and torture each other more viciously and maliciously than any member of the animal kingdom, have radically changed my perception of men. I'm terrified of what they are capable of.

Joy, who was always ahead of the times, knew she was on to a good thing with her tales of male cruelty and female submissiveness. She intuited that as women became more confident, better educated and more threatening, the more male sadism and brutality would sell. (And the easier it would be to get a still-patriarchal publishing world to want—unconsciously, once again, of course—to back her books.) And if she'd just stuck to straight violence and not added so much sick sex, her work would probably still be viable. Rape, torture and battering are still hot entertainment values. Isn't male violence the real star of the show of war films, *Miami Vice* and those beautifully art-directed films of Brian de Palma, not to mention the whole clobbering Rambo fantasy?

What is all this new, extravagant gore *for?*

Lots of people say it replaces the jollies people used to get from public hangings and floggings. Others claim it's the way we sublimate our post-industrial, post-modern mega-malaise. I say it's to scare the shit out of us.

I say the malevolent subtext of all that violence is "Look how vicious we are, girls. Just don't push us too far, girls."

YES SIR.

Whatever you say. Would you like me to make coffee? Lick your stamps? Your ass?

Listen, darlings, I think it's just wonderful that women with college educations and brilliant minds are also servants. I think it's divine that they must race home from work to cook dinner, sort the laundry and tidy up the day's mess. Women love doing twice as much work as men. Women hate relaxing. Women are more durable. Women are made to suffer. And if some get uppity, just knock them around a little, or threaten to, and you'll see, they'll do whatever it is you want them to do.

We had a Swedish maid when I was around eleven whose name was Hannah. She had run away from her husband, a drunk, who beat her regularly. When he came to the door one day to take her away with him, my mother threw him out. The salient fact here: He was afraid of my mother.

I wonder, is receiving welfare checks from a cold and resilient bureaucracy really more dignified and more liberating than working for a flesh-and-blood, middle-class wife and mother?

My mother was a good boss. Unlike the welfare system, she always encouraged whoever was working for her to have a savings account. Toward the end, she even occasionally borrowed from the maid. She also got them to the doctor when they were sick, told them her troubles and listened to theirs. As women go, my mother was rarely lonely. Neither was the person who worked for her.

But all that is past. Now, at the end of this woman-liberating century, working as a servant in someone's home is considered one of the most humiliating, degrading, disgusting jobs a person can have. Well below being a sanitation engineer or zoo worker.

If men didn't bring about all these changes *consciously*, what did? Some ghastly natural law that decrees that women must always be the world's main beast of burden? Is that why we accepted the loss of servants without a fight—not even a few harsh words?

Sometimes I think we really are as helpless as bugs, dictated to by some irrational compulsion that says women must be suppressed and overruled forever and that's all there is to it. Perhaps that's what my obsessive need to paint insects is all about.

* * *

Somehow writing these thoughts fills me with shame. How dare I, with my splendid apartment and gentle husband, complain that I don't have a full-time servant?

Because I am not complaining. I'm explaining.

Now that the children are grown I don't need or especially want someone else picking up after me. And I am fully aware, from an economic point of view, how lucky I am. I am where most women want to be.

I am also nearing middle age and it's a little late, I think, to give men a run for their money. I've been in service a pretty long time.

All I want to make clear in my own mind is that, no matter how terrific it looks up here in this stratosphere where I've landed, I'd like it to be better for Roberta. I don't want her ever to say "I need a wife."

I'd like to be able to tell her it will be different for her, but I doubt if it will be.

Men still hold the reins and are still more aggressive and violent than we are. And whatever they give us, they can also take away.

If they took away our servants yesterday, they can take away our freedom and education tomorrow. And if the great, calamitous depression economists are constantly predicting ever comes, women may well get back their servants, but there's no doubt in my mind that those bright, stunning, confident women competing with men in corporate boardrooms would be sent home.

The men, you see, would need the work more. And as we know, working people need a wife.

And on and on it goes. We lose a little dignity here, we get a little power there. But it always adds up to less dignity and power than theirs.

Unless, of course, one happens to be Marisa.

NINE

Just as I was getting ready to drag myself up to my studio today, Joy called and now everything has changed, been turned upside down and transmogrified into crisis and ambiguity. I am so stunned I can't paint. To get my thoughts in order and calm down, I am recording what happened exactly as Joy described it to me on the phone.

Apparently, Scott received a phone call from Franny Fagen of Towne Publishing yesterday.

It took him twenty-four hours to tell Joy. During that time, he took his telephone off the hook, hung the three pictures Marisa had given him, bought a large, expensive, mahogany-finish wooden file cabinet, typed out little labels, encased in clear, indestructible plastic, attached them to his numerous file folders and neatly arranged all his papers inside them.

He spent the rest of the day shopping for computers and signed up for a word processing course at the YMCA. On the way home, he bought a camel's hair sweater with suede elbow patches, not unlike the one he had seen the late John Cheever wearing in a book jacket photo.

Then he cooked a dinner of broiled fish, broccoli and boiled potatoes to which he did not invite Joy. Among other decisions he made that day, he is going to lose the ten pounds he gained since his affair with her began.

At nine A.M. today, he finally rings Joy's doorbell.

His face is clean shaven but his hair is interestingly tousled. Her face is puffy and pale. She has been sleeping heavily, having taken (she tells me) an over-the-counter, nonaddictive antihistamine sleeping tablet. Her nightgown is a shirt he has left behind in her apartment.

"That's my shirt" are his first words.

"I only wear it because I love you," she replies. "It makes me think about you while I go to sleep." She studies his chipper appearance. "Where were you all day yesterday? I tried to call you, but the line was always busy. Was your phone off the hook? Do you want some coffee?"

"I've already had breakfast."

"What's wrong? Why are you so cold acting? Are you angry with me?"

"No."

"You're going back to Marisa. That's it, isn't it?"

"No."

His two monosyllabic replies, straight in a row, give her a terrible sense of foreboding. Scott, after all, is her last hope. She steps back from the door. "Well, come on in, for God's sake, and tell me what's going on."

"I heard from Franny Fagen," he says as he enters her sunny, piteously underfurnished living room. "She read every word of my book and loves it."

"Terrific," she says bravely and sits down in the director's chair nearest her, taking care to fold the shirttails around her thighs so nothing in the nature of bumps or mottles shows in the bright morning light.

"She says she can make it a bestseller. She says the market is ripe for an explicitly male backlash book. She says everyone wants to hate the women's movement, and they especially want to hate a woman like Marisa." Then, smiling broadly, revealing the full extent of glee that is cavorting in his brain, he tells her about all the constructive things he did in his apartment the day before.

"Oh Scott, that's wonderful." She rises and throws her arms around him. The top button of her (his) shirt rips in the process and the upper half of her breasts is visible. She flattens them against the rough camel's hair sweater, but he barely seems to notice. "Oh God, you must be so happy. Sit down and tell me everything." She pushes his shoulders down hard and forces him into one of the living room's three director's chairs.

He crosses his legs and adjusts the crease in his trousers. "She's going to help me edit it down to a normal-size book."

"Did she say if she can get Towne to put some real money into promoting it?"

"Yes. She has already shown the last section, which she says is the best, to the director of subsidiary rights, whatever that is, and to the head of the sales department, and they both said the book's a winner."

"Oh, this is wonderful. All my feelings about your book have been validated. I'm so glad Franny listened to me. I knew from the start it was a super, super book."

"No, you didn't."

"What do you mean? Wasn't it me who sent the manuscript to her?"

"Yes, and I'm very grateful for that."

"I was the first person to believe in you."

"That's not what she told me."

"What did she tell you?"

"She said you said it was boring, self-indulgent and full of crap, and that she should let me down easy."

"She's lying. I never said it was self-indulgent or any of those things."

"She sounded pretty convincing to me."

"I said that *if she didn't like it,* she should let you down easy. And I only said that because I love you."

"Yes, I know."

"From the beginning, I said it had great commercial potential. I always said the portrait of Marisa was devastating and wonderful."

"Fine, well, I've got to go down to meet Franny this morning."

"But it's only nine o'clock. At least have some coffee. I've got some Entenmann's coffee cake. Wait, I'll just heat it up."

"No, thanks. She's coming in early. She wants to get started right away on the editing and work closely with me."

"You'll hate being with her all the time. She's enormous. She's got a big red face and walks around the office looking like a king-size unmade bed. And anyway, I should be the one to edit it. You promised me you'd let me edit it for you."

"No, I didn't."

"Please, Scott, don't cut me out like this."

"I've got to hurry. The subway will be crowded. Look, I'll call you soon."

"You're leaving me. I can feel it."

"Well, I'm leaving to go downtown. I'll talk to you later."

"I swear to you I never said anything negative about your book. I swear—"

She wants to get down on her knees, but her floors are bare and littered with the odd nut and stray penny. So she pulls at his sweater with one hand and coils the other around his neck. He moves away, fussily straightening his hair, and leaves the room to look at himself in the mirror hanging by the front door. "Do you like this sweater with a tie or should I just wear my shirt open at the collar?"

"Oh Scott, it doesn't matter. You look gorgeous either way. I'm just so glad for you. You're going to be famous. You're going to be rich. Why are you being so mean to me?"

"Am I being mean?" He puts his hand on the doorknob.

"I can't believe this. STOP."

"I've got to go." He kisses her on the nose and is gone.

Now this is a wonderful turn of events. I should be dancing in my living room and breaking open champagne. Circumstances beyond my control have brought my tale to a logical and proper conclusion: Joy, who wanted to exploit Scott, as she has exploited everyone else, has herself been exploited and dumped instead.

I, who nearly offered up my second husband to be her patsy, have been saved from my folly.

Worst of all (best of all): Joy has failed to manipulate her way out of trouble and will now be obliged to look clearly at her duplicity and see what a selfish, conniving person she is.

She has no one to turn to. She is completely alone. Justice has prevailed and she is being punished at last. Then why am I not happy?

Why am I almost as angry at Scott as she is? Why do I loathe him for writing his Marisa-hating book and insinuating his way into the good graces of the desperate Franny? Why am I still burning?

TEN

I've always thought that anger defines who you are and that fear is what limits you.

Anger comes straight from the gut and swells you up with a sense of your own being.

Fear negates. It makes you smaller—more sociable. Thank goodness. If each person's identity were allowed full rein, there would be such chaos we would never have developed beyond protozoa.

Nevertheless, anger is the best function and comes before fear. A baby's first cry is one of anger: a powerful assertion of self, an announcement that a demanding, important human being has just been born.

No mother on earth can ignore that first cry, that sure knowledge that not only has someone who must be taken care of just entered her life, but someone to reckon with.

I don't know when I put together this theory. Probably after a temper tantrum I had at school. (I never had temper tantrums at home. Rage was something our harmonious family didn't harbor.)

I had been passed over for an art prize but I believed in my work enough to thunder at my art teacher for ten minutes.

I remember thinking, even while I was ranting, This is the real me. This is saying what the real me wants and has earned, and I felt exultant.

My teacher listened in silence and never reported me. The next semester I got the first prize. I had won.

This triumph frightened me and still frightens me a little, which is why, much as I honor my anger, I so rarely express it.

But surely I am straying from the point. What has all this to do with Scott and Joy and why do I now distrust him? Where once I had seen only dullness and simple opportunism, why do I now see craftiness and greed?

Something has happened inside me to bring out all this formless rage, which, contrary to my theory, is not telling me anything at all. It is almost as much a mystery to me as my new sympathy for Joy.

Joy has had dinner at our apartment three nights in a row. I even let her come to the dinner party we had on Tuesday for Hank Leary, the great real-estate developer. She was very good. No mention of orgies or beatings, just a few words about Maddy Bolingbroke's stage fright and her father's kind understanding of the problem. Old Hank, who grew up in Hell's Kitchen, was completely taken in by her and salivating for more celebrity anecdotes, but she went silent long before the dessert. Her heart simply wasn't in it.

She is acting like a broken bird and pitiful to watch. Her YSL suits are wrinkled and spotted. The blond wisps of hair around her face look darker, oilier.

She is wretched and passive and pointless. I want to shake her, tell her she has been a sap to trust the red-faced Franny Fagen and to have given so much to Scott.

If it hadn't been for Joy, his long-winded, self-pitying, misogynist book would have stayed buried at the bottom of the slush pile forever. The size alone would have been reason enough for an editor to ignore it forever.

And it's trash. I know it's trash. Franny knows it is too. She is buying it and will work herself to death to edit it because she longs to have a man for herself. Joy said she would see right away that it was by someone who had just become available on the marriage market and would understand why she, Joy, was pushing the book. Well, did she ever! She understood so well she decided to haul in Scott for herself.

I have never met this enormous Franny, who walks around looking like an unmade bed, but I have no trouble picturing her nail-bitten, fat-fingered hands giddily flipping through his manuscript, eagerly searching for signs of commercial promise, hoping against hope that she can turn his tirade against his beautiful, intelligent, wealthy wife into salable fiction and get this man into her bed.

"And the worst part is she probably can make it good," Joy said yesterday afternoon, sitting mournfully before me in our living room. Her amber-colored eyes were filled with tears. The lights reflecting off them made me think of amber's fossilized bugs. "She's a frustrated writer and a brilliant editor and oh God, maybe his book *is* good."

"How much did you actually read of it?" I asked.

"Not as much as I should have," she said, removing a little Shalimar atomizer from her purse and squirting herself with it.

"How much?"

"At least the first ninety pages. And they were hideous. How was I to know the rest wasn't?" She moaned. "I forgot that a lot of first novelists learn how to write as they go along and their endings are much better than their beginnings. Apparently Franny thinks the last five hundred pages are a tour de force. But no professional, responsible editor would have waded through the first fifteen hundred pages before they found the good stuff. Only real lust could have kept Franny reading. And real hate for me, which I don't deserve."

"Did you ever do anything to make her dislike you?"

"No. I promise you, no. Years ago, when I was still a top-selling writer, she used to take me out for three-course luncheons at The Four Seasons and charge them to Towne. She wanted me to do a book for Towne. She liked me. She used to go out with Fred Worth and we laughed together about him after I divorced him."

"You didn't take Fred away from her or anything, did you?"

"Of course not," she hollered, rising from the sofa, standing in the center of the room and all but stamping her foot. "They had an affair centuries ago and broke up long before I married him. Look, I'm telling you she was my *friend*."

She paced around the room, slamming down her bangs with one hand, jabbing at the cuticles of the other and nearly knocking over the Brancusi when she passed it. It was five o'clock. Kenneth would be home soon. He was putting up with her presence every evening with difficulty. He thought Scott's dumping Joy was completely appropriate. Maybe there is a God after all, is what he said when I told him about Franny, the book and Scott.

If, when he came home from work, he found her hollering and stomping around the living room, his tolerance could well reach its limit.

I managed to get her out of the apartment before he returned, but signs of her presence were everywhere: in the lipstick-stained sherry glass, the mound of tear-filled Kleenexes in the waste basket and the heavy scent of Shalimar on the sofa.

"Why do you let that woman come over here?" Kenneth demanded when he got home and had seen her little trail of clues.

"Because I feel sorry for her."

"How can you? She broke up your marriage. She used you. She tried to use me." His suit and hair were unrumpled, as neat and clean as his logical, cause-and-effect mind. Which, in the final analysis, I respect, but this wasn't the moment for logic.

"I know it seems ridiculous to you, but I'm madder at Scott than I've ever been with her."

"Why?"

"I don't know why. I just am. I am furious he's cashing in on his hatred for his ex-wife," I said or probably snarled. I sank my hands into my hair and pulled at the roots. Anger—irrational, inappropriate—was pouring out of me like dragon fire. I wanted to mumble curses and tear at my clothes.

It was none of my business and uncalled for, but that's how it was and how I felt.

"I'm going for a walk," I announced and, before he could say another word, I grabbed my purse and ran out of the living room. But not before noticing the odd, pursed-mouth look on Kenneth's face.

As if he were confirming a long-ignored suspicion that women were creeps and fools and that he had married one of the creepiest and most foolish.

It was six o'clock and still light when I stepped out onto the pavement of our building and realized that it was a balmy spring evening. A sweet, puffy breeze was swaying the wide, budding green trees lining the street.

I headed toward Central Park. Normally, I never go into the park in the evening. I am afraid of muggers and rapists and having my breasts lopped off and thrown in the bushes. But anger expands, and suddenly the city seemed safer and more benevolent. Nothing bad could happen to me with such a fine warm rage inside me.

If I walked at a good clip, I could cross the park in fifteen minutes. From there, I could stroll along Central Park West to 107th Street, then turn left to Broadway.

By the time I got to Scott's shabby building, I would have burned off the more ferocious parts of my anger, maybe even arrived at some understanding of where it came from, and would be able to confront him with something like his own icy control.

ELEVEN

"But I have done nothing to you, Madeleine. None of what you're saying makes any sense. You do realize that, don't you?"

He tiptoed around his desk, a solid, shining mahogany affair, and put his hand on my shoulder. The camel's hair sweater contrasted nicely with his thick black hair. He was clean shaven, and looked well rested and healthy. Above all, he was serene.

His apartment was immaculate and the soft reds in the Kelim rug on the living-room floor blended nicely with his brown sofas. Marisa's paintings, dismissed by Joy as some sort of brownish things, were three rather interesting abstracts by Adolph Gottlieb. In the bookshelves, I spotted the works of Dickens and other classics.

He sat down on the sofa opposite me, legs apart, hands folded, and studied me. He looked like an ethologist studying an animal in the wild. "Now, let's go over the facts again," he said in the voice of someone who has decided a calm assertion of authority is the only defense under the circumstances.

"I know the facts. You gave Joy your book and she gave it to Towne and now you're breaking up with her."

"No, let's start from the beginning. Joy went to bed with your first husband," he said softly, making a little tent with his hands.

"What does that have to do with it? That was years ago. Who told you?"

"She did."

"Okay. So she did sleep with him. He never really loved me and she helped accelerate the breakup of what was already a bad marriage."

"And before that, didn't you lend her your apartment so she could write there on weekends?"

"She told you that too? What's so awful about it? I did a kind deed. She was grateful. Period."

"I know she was grateful. She told me she was. She gave it as an example of your goodness of heart."

"Well, I am good-hearted."

"So am I."

"No, you're not. How can you say that when you've used her as you used Marisa?"

Anger, possibly brutality—the ethologist who also has a gun—snaked across his face. His hands tightened their grasp of each other. Lowering his eyes, he sat there breathing at the floor for a few minutes without speaking. Finally, he looked up. "Marisa has nothing to do with any of this."

I didn't reply. I was beginning to realize that, for me, she had everything to do with it.

"I think you should put this whole thing into perspective. First of all, Joy was trying to manipulate me just as she had manipulated you. I saw it in so many ways. She was completely transparent."

"Of course she was. She trusted you."

He snorted. "She trusted me to support her for the rest of her life and even pay her income taxes."

"What's so terrible about that? You liked each other, didn't you? She was helping you with your book."

"Just like she helped Frederick Worth."

"What does Joy's ex-husband have to do with this?"

"I can see you haven't grasped the whole soap opera."

"No, I guess not."

"Franny was in love with Frederick. And she has always resented Joy for getting Frederick on drugs and destroying his acting career."

"That's a lie. Franny courted Joy. She wanted her to do a book for Towne. She constantly took her out to lunch at The Four Seasons."

"That's possible. Franny is too good a businesswoman to let her personal feelings get in the way of pursuing a best-selling author. But the truth is, she loved Fred Worth and has never forgiven Joy for what she did to him. And she fears, quite rightly, that Joy would do the same to me."

"Of course she'd say that to you if she hates Joy. But I don't believe for a minute that she was brokenhearted over Frederick Worth."

"Well, she was and she sees no reason to turn down my book, which, by the way, is a very good book, as a favor to Joy. Unlike you, she did not want to be used by Joy again."

"What do you mean 'again'? Joy hasn't used me again. Unless you call my giving her a few free meals using me. Other than that—what? Kenneth didn't get you a job."

"She's using you right now by getting you all worked up over my book, which, frankly, is no concern of yours. She probably even has you hating Franny too."

"Not at all. I simply came here to tell you that I think you treated Joy shittily. What difference if she's a con artist? That's how she thinks. And anyhow, she's small time compared to you and she's lost her touch. She's run out of people to exploit. But you, you never will."

He rose, turned his back to me and fiddled with some

papers, tidily piled on the desk. "Well, that's about it. There's nothing more to say."

His abrupt change of manner infuriated me. "Am I being dismissed?" I bellowed. "Have you had enough of me now?"

He swung around. Face red. Square body roiling with muscles. "I want you to leave. Yes." Heat was pouring out of him. I could *feel* the temperature in the room rise.

I picked up my purse. "Fine. It's your apartment. Your book. Your betrayal. I just wanted to make my views known."

A pusillanimous retreat, but he was frightening to behold. "Then go."

The tone, the words, were like a switch.

"I HAVEN'T FINISHED YET," I roared. My legs were trembling, but suddenly blood—fantastic, happy, strong blood, loaded with adrenaline—was rushing through me. My head was full of it. My lungs were swelling. At last, I was thinking straight, seeing clearly.

"I *agree* Joy manipulates people," I shouted. "I agree she's scheming. I *agree,* but I'm finally realizing that's just one way some women have to operate: through tricks and cheating. But no matter how much she connives, she isn't the enemy. She never was. And though I can't stand her for using me, and yes, I think I am a more talented, serious artist than she and probably you will ever be, that is not the problem. The problem is no matter whether you're a true-blue, heart-of-gold housewife like me or a conniver like Joy, we lose. We end up being used.

"And listen, I don't hate Franny. I feel sorry for her because she'll edit your book and promote you at Towne and spread her legs and beg you to fuck her, and cook your breakfast and take your suits to the cleaners, but, no matter what she does for you, she'll end up being discarded in the end, either because she made you famous and you don't need her anymore or because she didn't and you need someone else.

"And more than anything, I love Marisa. I love knowing

that a beautiful woman like her, with money and servants, exists. A woman who can become an anthropologist and still have terrific children and isn't obliged to stay with a man she no longer loves or clean up the bathroom after him. I'd worship at her feet if I could. Because she won't and didn't ever degrade herself for you. We need her, us schmucks down here in reality, who get taken into male households to serve. Like me. *Me*. Ask Kenneth. Call him up and tell him to come and get his schmuck wife who is in your apartment screaming at you."

I sat down. I'd said I was screaming, but I'd long since stopped. My diatribe had taken on the dull, angst-ridden rhythms of some eternal, misery-loving chorus. The old, familiar woman's lament. Men win. Women lose. Unless they have money. And even then. Even then, they manage to lose most of the time.

"Go ahead. Call Kenneth. You know, man-to-man. Tell him, Look, I can't get your wife out of here. She's making a racket. Take her home and lock her up."

"You really want me to call him?" Those were his only words. I had been at him for at least ten minutes but, secure master animal that he was, he had allowed me to carry on. Why not amuse oneself watching this smaller creature howl? It wouldn't attack. It knew enough not to go after a beast stronger and more violent than itself. It knew enough to fear.

But fear limits.

Fear negates. And this is what fear tells me: I am the weaker, not the fiercer, animal. I do not draw the line which I toe. *And I hate it.*

But fear also socializes. Because of fear, I've been supported by two men who have helped raise my children and paid for my paints and canvases. Fed me. Fucked me. Put money in my little bank account. Fear teaches you how to get along.

And Joy? Not enough fear. Like a monkey full of tricks

and daring who, through craft and stealth, darts back and forth over the line.

But not Marisa. She is beyond fear and anger. She is mythic. She is blessed.

I never want to meet her. I want her to remain a legend in my mind, a glorious being beyond male power, like Eurynome, like Artemis or Isis. Where have they all gone? Why, after two thousand years of Christianity, is the only notable woman left in heaven the beleaguered, sexually deprived Mary?

Poor madonna. Dear little virgin. Giving birth in a stable. Fleeing to Egypt. Anguish and suffering throughout her whole sad, marginal life. Did she ever rebel? Not on your life. She got down on her knees and worshiped her son.

Scott shifted in his chair. I looked up and saw that his face was filled with something akin to sympathy. The last rays of the sun coming through the freshly washed windows had settled in his thick black hair. "Franny loves the Marisa character too. That's one of the reasons she liked my book."

"I don't believe that."

"It's true."

"Joy told me you made Marisa a bitch. She said it was a male backlash book, that Franny said the market was ready to hate a wealthy woman like Marisa."

"Joy got it wrong. In fact, Marisa is only one of many women characters in the book. There are lots of male characters too."

"Whom Marisa mistreats?"

"Not at all. She's a nice person. Though I'm afraid she's not as beautiful as you seem to think she is. Especially when she gets a sty in her eye."

"She gets sties?"

"Mmm. Big red ones."

"Because she obviously sees too much."

"Or doesn't clean her contact lenses. She also talks constantly. I've had fun with that in the book."

"I bet you have."

"But over all, I've made her very sympathetic. Ask Franny. And the book is far from being anti-woman. It's an attempt to get at the truth and be objective."

"So what you're saying is that Joy lied?" The question was rhetorical. For by then I knew she had, that she would *always* lie.

He shrugged resignedly. "She's very good at it."

"Oh Lord, I feel like such a fool."

"She had me completely seduced too. At least during the first month I knew her," he said.

"I was really beginning to see through her conniving and was even toying with ways to punish her. She knew I was on to her and *still* she was able to manipulate me and make me feel what she wanted me to feel."

"She probably intuited how you felt about Marisa and used that to stir you up," he said. "She figured it would motivate you to help her get back on her feet. Now that I've turned out to be a dead end, she needs you more than ever."

"Tell me, was it also a lie that you hated Marisa having servants?"

"Why would I hate having servants?"

"She said you wanted Marisa to cook your breakfast."

"Believe me, Madeleine, the servants were not the problem. They helped rather than hindered our marriage."

"Then why did you break up with her?"

"I don't really owe you an answer to that question." He sighed, shifted his weight in his chair and, for a moment, looked like the tired old man he would sooner or later become. "And I'm not really sure why. Maybe . . . maybe the real reason is I just prefer to be alone."

I gazed around the apartment. Yes, a loner. Everything

from the orderly desk and file cabinets to the dark, polished floor reflected self-sufficiency and a tightly organized psyche.

Nevertheless, he was nice. And the cushions on the sofa were filled with goose down and soft.

"What makes me really mad at myself," I went on, "is that I was plotting with her to get you to marry her or at least support her. I felt so *sorry* for her."

"Do you want a drink?"

"Do I look like I need one?"

"No. I'd just like you to stay a while." He smiled and kept smiling until I managed a weak grin of my own.

"Some vodka, please, if you have it."

He walked to the kitchen and made noises with ice trays while I searched in my purse to see if I had enough money to take a cab home. And then I remembered I had taken my wallet out and left it on my kitchen counter when I had tipped the grocery delivery boy.

I closed my eyes. I was so tired. I wanted to sleep and sleep forever, see the past with headlights flaring across the backyard, through the kitchen door and into our old Elm Street house of many harmonies.

When did my mother lose her anger? And my poor father, so broke and fearful in the end. Fear fools you into thinking that appearances can protect you. But they protect you from none of life's facts.

And no doubt Joy was right. Part of me was indeed like some Agnes Moorehead character. Dour and bitter, locking up emotions my parents didn't allow themselves or their children to express. All of us jangling our dungeon keys.

He returned with two glasses full of ice and carried them to the bar table. "Tonic?"

"No, straight."

He poured my drink and handed it to me with a cocktail napkin tucked under the glass. His movements were swift and efficient, those of a man who knew how to take care of himself.

He looked down at me with interest. "So what are you concluding?"

Did he really still want to know what I thought? Hadn't I said it all and wasn't it all more of the same boring feminist ranting?

"I've concluded—" My voice cracked. I was going to cry. Like Joy. Like some miserable slave. I shoved the glass into my mouth and poured vodka on my quavering vocal cords. It burned, but the weepiness stopped. "I've concluded that, when all is said and done, I'd rather have been born a man."

I said that. I still can't believe I did. I don't know why. Possibly because I trusted him. I'm not sure if I feel guilty, sniveling or glad I said it. In any event, it was—at that moment—the truth.

He shook his head kindly. The professor noticing the wild animal's irrepressible cuteness as it buries its head in its paws and admits to the most shameful of longings: to be the biggest, fiercest beast in the forest.

"Well, I'd like to be Marisa," he said.

"Marisa?"

"If I were to be reincarnated, that is."

I stared at him, amazed. What kind of man was this?

"Do you know about goddesses?" I asked cautiously.

"Goddesses? Like Venus and Diana?"

"Yes, but I'm thinking more of the big, powerful goddesses in the most ancient myths that no one ever talks about. Like Eurynome or Nut, the Egyptian goddess of the sky, or Nammu from Sumerian legends. The ones who people used to think created the world."

"Like in the Robert Graves theory about the White Goddess?"

"*Not* a theory. There's *proof* that in prehistoric times people believed in a supreme goddess. She's in all the great oral legends." I paused and waited for him to sigh with boredom. But he didn't. He was listening.

I swirled the ice in my glass and stretched my feet out. I was beginning to relax. Not a lot. But enough.

"What really has me baffled, though," I went on, "is how men can have worshiped an all-powerful goddess when women have been subservient for so many thousands of years. Even now, reading in the papers about all the wife beating or about Moslems making women go back to the veil and Afghan women still having clitorectomies, I begin to think female suppression is the natural *law*. And that we really are programmed by DNA—or whatever—to be browbeaten forever. That we're as powerless over our destiny as the insects I keep painting."

His head jerked up, his eyes alive with thought. "But if people believed in powerful goddesses once, that shows, doesn't it, that there is no natural law that says women must be treated like inferiors?"

"How?"

"It proves societies can reverse themselves and no, men are not programmed to tyrannize women forever and ever. They've just done it during the six-thousand-year patch of history we know about."

He raised his glass to me in a toast. "So, here's to the next millennium."

"Sounds lovely. I wish I were convinced."

"Look at how Americans changed their minds about blacks. Thirty years ago they were still talking about them as some sort of subspecies and now they're electing them mayors."

"Maybe that's why I like blacks so much. They inspire me." I took another gulp of vodka. "But just because they've more or less succeeded doesn't mean we will."

"But you might," he murmured absently.

"You must find all this very tedious."

"Not at all. The human mind is endlessly malleable." His eyes had left mine. He was staring up at the ceiling, lost in another thought. Was it something to do with his book? With me? Whatever it was, the problems of women seemed to have vacated his mind.

I waited politely for whatever was preoccupying him to pass and looked at the attractive brass light fixture above him. It had eight brass arms and parchment shades. The building never would have provided it. He would have had to install it himself.

Finally, he turned back to me. "I was thinking about reincarnation again. I just realized that I also wouldn't mind coming back as an old-fashioned hobo. You know, eating baked beans down by the railroad yard."

"They were gay. Haven't you read about them in Hemingway's short stories?"

"Well, I'd like to be a non-gay one."

"I wonder if all loners have that dream."

He laughed. Being called a loner seemed to please him. He eyed me mischievously. "In a way, though, I understand your wish. To be a man, I mean. I'd rather not be an artist working out of my husband's home and not exactly breaking the bank. But you may someday. And you have a pretty good life. You have kids. Joy tells me you're very proud of them."

"I am."

"So? You're not bereft."

"Men have kids too."

"Well, I rather like you as you are. Men don't have your looks."

"My looks are not part of this discussion. My looks go with being a woman. No more, no less."

"Well, I like them."

"Thank you."

"And I like listening to you say how you feel."

"Oh goodie. Can I be in your next book?"

"When are you going to stop?" he asked quietly. His eyes, which are navy blue, turned soft. They looked like velvety sapphire pillows, full of understanding and insinuations. A woman could lose herself in them for a long, long time. Joy had been so busy trying to use him she probably never even noticed his eyes, just as she had never noticed the quality of the books on his shelves. But then, what con artist ever respects or sees anything admirable in her mark?

He raised his right hand, as if to reach across the space between us and stroke me. But something changed his mind. Perhaps the space was too far to reach. Perhaps he feared I would rebuff him.

Fear limits.

And yet, we want, all of us, so much to love.

"I can't finish this drink," I said, as wary as he. "I should go home, but I left without my wallet. Could you lend me some money for a cab?"

"Of course I can. But do you have to go now? While you're still upset?"

"I'm not upset. I've said all I've had to say. I can go home now and spend the rest of my life thinking about it."

"Madeleine?"

"Yes."

Silence. He was shy. That evening at the Metropolitan Club, I'd interpreted his shyness as stiffness. And I hadn't given him credit for having anything under it but opportunism. But of course, I had seen him only from Joy's point of view. And all the time, under that shy mask, there might well have been nothing but straightforward striving.

Striving to get at some human truth which Franny Fagen has recognized. Which explained the fear I sensed in him that evening. And explained my own deepest fear too.

People striving to get at the truth are always afraid. We

fear we won't find it and if we do, we won't have the courage to express it.

I got up and crossed the few feet between us. My hand on his shoulder. My heart pounding. It is not my habit to cross the space between me and others. "Look, I'm sorry. I'm sorry I yelled at you."

He touched my hand lightly and looked away. He didn't trust me. For good reason. But surely I could dislodge his suspicions. If I sank into the cushions beside him. If I put my arms around him. If I pulled his body against mine.

And then we heard the key scraping in the lock. First the top bolt turned. The wrong way. Then the bottom lock. Also the wrong way. She jiggled the doorknob, realized her error and began again. We watched her struggle in silence. Only when the door opened did I take my hand off his shoulder.

"Whew!" Joy said as she entered. "I simply can't work that lock. Hi, Scott. Hi, Madeleine."

"Hi," we both said.

"I came to tell Scott I'm going out to the Coast, but as long as you're here, Madeleine, I can kill two birds with one stone." She was wearing the white Victorian nightdress and cameo.

Her poise and command of the situation were superb. Not a trace of surprise or indignation upon seeing me in Scott's apartment.

"Can I get you a drink?" Scott asked.

"Some Perrier, thanks."

He rose and walked into the kitchen as if he were glad to get away from her, if only for a minute or two.

"I was invited out to L.A. by my sister," she said while waiting for Scott to return. "She's paying for my ticket. She's done very well for herself in the past two years. She wants me to see her house and pool and meet her new husband. He's a TV producer. I thought, Why not? I need a change."

"Does she have children?" I asked.

"Two boys by her first marriage."

"So that's good. Nephews are fun. You're not responsible for them and you can just enjoy them."

"Mmmm." It was as if our conversation about her wanting children had never happened.

Scott returned with the Perrier. "When are you going?"

"From this apartment?"

"To California."

"Day after tomorrow. I'm putting my furniture in storage and giving up my apartment before they evict me." She sat down and fluffed her hair. It had been washed and the feathery curls tickling her forehead were full of their usual pep. Everything in her demeanor indicated that she had cut her losses and was moving on to sunnier, western pastures. "My sister's husband is talking about doing a mini-series based on *Fate Kisses Back.* Are you two an item now?"

The announcement and the question were so skillfully blended they could have been written into a sitcom.

"No, we're not an item," I replied quickly. "I came over here to yell at Scott for using you and that's what I did."

"And?"

"And then I stopped. Just a few minutes before you arrived."

"Just stopped?"

"Yes."

TWELVE

Four months have gone by since that night at Scott's.

Kenneth is designing a shopping mall in the Hudson valley which the local planning societies are fighting, but I know it will go through. Harold has gone to Spain for a special studies summer program. And Roberta is in New Hampshire working as a counselor at her old summer camp. In between seeing real-estate agents in the Hamptons about buying land, I'm going to the Art Students League. I've enrolled in a life class and am learning all over again how to draw figures.

Joy is in California writing a new script for *Fate Kisses Back*—the same book upon which Frederick Worth immolated his career and savings. Since she has never written a movie script before, she is working closely with her brother-in-law, who is the teensiest bit tired of her sister.

"He's so cute, Madeleine," she told me this morning when she called me from California. "A real teddy bear, with a bushy gray beard and a round, puffy stomach. I just want to squeeze him until he squeaks."

"Do you?"

"A little. Oh God, my sister would kill me if she knew." It was midnight her time, three A.M. my time, but not to worry. I wasn't sleeping anyhow. I'm not sleeping at all well these days. I've been thinking too much.

"You know, your sister just may," I said.

"What?"

"Kill you."

"Don't say that. You're giving me goose bumps."

"Why not? Sooner or later someone is going to get so angry at you they may well haul off and . . ."

"Thanks a lot."

"But I never will. I promise. Now that I understand you, I don't have it in my heart to do you in. And in a way, I admire you for getting as far as you have. And I think that it's wonderful they're making a movie of your book."

"A mini-series, not a movie, which is better because you reach a larger audience and sell more paperbacks."

"Tell me, have you spoken to Scott?" I asked.

"No, never after that night we were both there in his apartment." She didn't ask if I had seen him again. It didn't interest her.

When, after she had finished her Perrier at Scott's, I had demanded to know why she had told me his book was against Marisa, it didn't occur to her to apologize. "I guess I misunderstood" was all she said, her voice pitched as high as a five-year-old's. "It was all so confusing when Scott told me he sold it to Franny. I was so upset and he was rushing out to see her." And so on, with much straightening of her Victorian petticoats and patting of her freshly coiffed hair.

"Aren't you curious to know what the last five hundred pages of his book are like?" I asked this morning.

"No. Not especially." It was as if he had left the earth to trek around outer space. Nor, come to think of it, did she mention her sister's children. You'd have thought for someone dying to be a mother . . . but then, saying how much she wanted children was just another way to make me feel sorry for her, as well as privileged and superior to her. And consequently guilty. Her strategy doesn't really ever change, only the content and words do.

"So Scott's out of your life just like that?" I asked.

"I guess that's just how it goes."

"So you're on the road again. Well, think about what I said though. Watch out."

"Jesus!"

But nothing will happen to Joy. I've overdramatized her situation. There are hundreds and thousands of women like her circulating around our fifty states, capitalizing on their martyrdom, inspiring guilt, flattering and turning a profit for themselves.

She is not unique. She is of a kind. A very durable kind. She is the quintessential slave. Nietzsche got it wrong when he said Christians—who at least have some idea of goodness and loyalty despite their attachment to meekness and authority—are the main proponents of a slave morality. It's people like Joy who are. And the tragic thing is that most of them are women.

Even more tragic, their technique is pretty effective. It's a viable way to make a living. And though Joy may be down now, for a long time she had fun. She was smart enough to figure out that a show of female masochism got her men, women, free apartments, trips to the Caribbean and many, many meals. It was also hot commercial stuff, and during her best writing years she wrung every possible nickel out of it.

But all her talk of suffering was a smoke screen to cover up a will of iron in a poor girl whose parents were dead and who was determined to live well and famously. It never occurred to her that respect and dignity were possible for women, so she never went after them.

When I started writing, my aim was to find out why, more than any other friend, Joy disturbed me so much. And I guess

I have found my answer. There is no real Joy. For, more than anything else, she is a reflection of what you want to hear, whether it's tales of celebrities' sins, female submissiveness or clever feminist arguments. Whatever you want, she'll dish it out, as long as she knows you'll pay up in the end.

If I hadn't tried to help her ensnare Scott and gone this one last round with her—on this one last joy ride—I never would have understood this much about her. If she hadn't gotten me so enraged for Marisa's sake—for the sake of the myth I'd created about her—I never would have gone over to Scott's apartment and found out she had lied about his book, nor realized that I'd been conned again. I would have always kept hoping she would reveal something about herself that was fixed and true. But she didn't. Perhaps none of us can. So I'll never know the whole picture—how she sees herself, for instance. But I've found out enough.

And having done so, there didn't seem much point in writing about her anymore, so I stopped. I haven't been near my desk, or hardly thought about her, until she called this morning.

I have, however, been thinking about Marisa a great deal. After spending so many hours deploring Joy's poses and subterfuges, I suppose it's inevitable that I end up taking refuge in a fantasy of a woman who is her opposite in every way. A woman who never needs to manipulate, inspire guilt, flatter or reflect back other people's opinions. Who is just what she is.

For, in spite of Marisa's sties and her tendency to talk too much—which I prefer not to think about—I still see her as something wonderful. As a symbol, if you like, of glory. And power too.

Whether she wears contact lenses or is fixated on high-fiber diets is really beside the point. What matters is my dream of her and my discovery of a truth that may carry me through the rest of my life: It didn't occur to me to want to be a man when I let my mind wander around in thoughts of Marisa.

I felt uplifted. In other words, the opposite of how I felt when I thought about Joy or the sorrowful Mary collapsing at the foot of the cross, or any of the other female stars and martyrs who people my Western imagination. The drunks and glamorous suicides: Marilyn Monroe, Sylvia Plath, Zelda Fitzgerald, Cleopatra and Lady Hamilton. Crazy loners like Catherine the Great and Joan of Arc. Deluded, extravagant idiots like Marie Antoinette and Mary, Queen of Scots. Not to mention a whole train of fictional suicides and romantic fools in novels and operas: Anna Karenina, Emma Bovary, Daisy Miller, Holly Golightly, Blanche DuBois, Madame Butterfly, Lulu and all those Wagnerian sopranos who leap off cliffs or otherwise sacrifice themselves for their lovers.

Opera irritates me the most of all. Why must Mimi and Violetta and Manon be so relentlessly pitiful? Why does Carmen have to die ignobly at the hand of her lover while the infinitely more promiscuous Don Giovanni gets to stride boldly into hell?

Why are there so few real heroines anywhere to embolden us, perhaps cheer us up? No wonder women are victims, not just of men, but of all those stories of weak, downtrodden women.

But it's logical, I suppose. Men learned to write long before we did. While we stayed bound in our illiterateness—rearing children, cooking, nurturing, cleaning and tending to the needs of men—they had the time and the leisure to discover the "word." Which they called "the beginning." And it was— for them. But it was the end of those powerful, majestic goddesses whose long-ago glory still manages to filter through whenever I dream about Marisa.

They came out of *oral* legends, from a dark, primitive time when neither men nor women knew how to write, when women, perhaps, still had a voice and sat by the fire singing tales about their own mighty goddesses who, in addition to creating the world, refrained from committing suicide, drinking too much or dying in disgrace.

People make gods in their own image.

So, of course, it's clear and understandable why Western men exalted their male gods in their writings and banished ours, till no one was left in the heavens but the meek and suffering Mary, supported by a multitude of famous earthly and fictional female losers.

But how can we blame ourselves for respecting men's ability to write and eventually buying their idea of a male god whose history and attributes were inscribed on sacred stones and housed in golden temples? How could we, illiterates that we were, not be impressed by all that pomp, wealth and power?

And how can anyone not understand why Joy invented herself as a victim—and why I believed her—when victimhood has been the acceptable tradition for women for thousands of years?

But all that is behind us. We read now. We paint and write. If we fear or bow to male gods (human or otherwise) and still view women as flawed, pitiful martyrs and servants, it's our own fault. We've come too far to be buried by men's version of the cosmos.

Scott was right. Societies *do* change and the human mind is infinitely malleable. There never was and never will be any monstrous natural law that says women must be the servants of the earth forever. We are not ants forced into anthills or hornets crammed into nests. And I will never paint bugs again.

Since all these thoughts are new to me, I guess my wish that Joy finally give something to me has been fulfilled. For it was only because I started thinking about her self-disgracing ways and pain-loving heroines that I began to question all female heroines and see what a miserable bunch most of them were. Which in the end led me to Marisa in her house of sunlight and flowers.

It was also through Joy that I discovered my rage. And through Scott too. He helped.

I was curious to know how he was doing up there in his red and brown sanctuary, typing his masterpiece, all alone, in his elbow-patched sweater. Since I didn't want to talk to him directly, I called Mary Farrar, Joy's old literary agent, about four weeks ago. After telling her all about Scott and Joy's affair and his subsequent dumping of her when he sold his book to Towne, I asked her if she could find out what had happened with his book. Was Franny Fagen still hot for it? His body?

Since Mary still can't resist meddling in anything remotely to do with Joy, she went to work immediately and invited Franny to lunch.

The latter could speak of nothing but Scott all through the lunch. She is confident that once he has winnowed his book down to 350 pages, he'll be the next king of the bestseller lists.

When I asked Mary what Franny looked like, I wasn't surprised to find out that Joy's description of her had been a touch misleading. Apparently, Franny is quite slim. Though she is tall and tends to blush easily, she is not red faced and definitely not enormous. And her grooming the day they had lunch—tailored suit, button earrings, sleek silk blouse—has nothing to do with unmade beds. "She looks to be headed straight for the boardroom" is how Mary put it.

I was tempted to mention this last to Joy when she called, but now that my reputation for good-heartedness seems so well established in her mind, I am loath to disabuse her.

Unfortunately, Mary could not find out whether Scott and his editor are sleeping together. Blabbing about her affairs with authors is not, it seems, part of Franny's game plan. So I'll never know if any of my predictions about them will come true, which is probably better.

Part of me would like to call Scott and ask to read the whole two thousand pages before they get winnowed. I would especially like to read all the parts concerning Marisa that he edits out.

But I haven't called him and don't intend ever to call him. I'm afraid that if the book is good, as he says it is, I'll risk wanting to see him again, maybe loving him. But if it's bad and his "objectivity" about Marisa leads him to the same, tiresome chauvinism of so many men's novels, I might hate him. Neither of which emotions I intend to harbor since I happen to love and enjoy living with Kenneth, who, I believe, loves me too. And for all my new awareness about goddesses and violence, I am not a loner. And neither is Kenneth.

Therefore I will do nothing about Scott. I will let him and his book be. Because this morning, I've found out what I unconsciously wanted to find ever since I started writing about Joy.

I know what I'm going to do now that my children are grown and my period of full-time service is almost over. I would like to change the world—most midwesterners would—but since I can't, I'll do the best I can.

I'm going to paint Marisa. Not the real-life Marisa. I never want to meet her. She must remain distant forever. But always there. Large, mythic, bold. On acres of lawn, with acolytes gathering flowers, bringing her nectar, combing her hair.

Five years from now, maybe I'll have a little show in Bridge-hampton. If I'm lucky, it will be at the Benson, which is in an old wood-frame building with a gallery that opens out onto a garden.

One hot summer evening, perhaps there will be an opening with a modest crowd in polo shirts and sneakers, crossing and recrossing the courtyard, sipping wine from plastic glasses, looking at the prices before they look at the pictures.

And what they'll see is Marisa, the beauty, who is also a scholar, riding through fields of wildflowers. A woman who inspires neither guilt nor pity. Who is never a victim and never a fool.

She must never leave my imagination.

We need her too much in this world of Joys.